JERSEY
LEGENDS

ERREN MICHAELS

JERSEY LEGENDS

For my mum

First published 2015

The History Press
The Mill, Brimscombe Port
Stroud, Gloucestershire, GL5 2QG
www.thehistorypress.co.uk

Text © Erren Michaels, 2015
Illustrations © Jeremy Harrison & Erren Michaels, 2015

British Library Cataloguing in Publication Data.
A catalogue record for this book is available from the British Library.

ISBN 978 0 7509 6588 0

Typesetting and origination by The History Press
Printed in Great Britain

CONTENTS

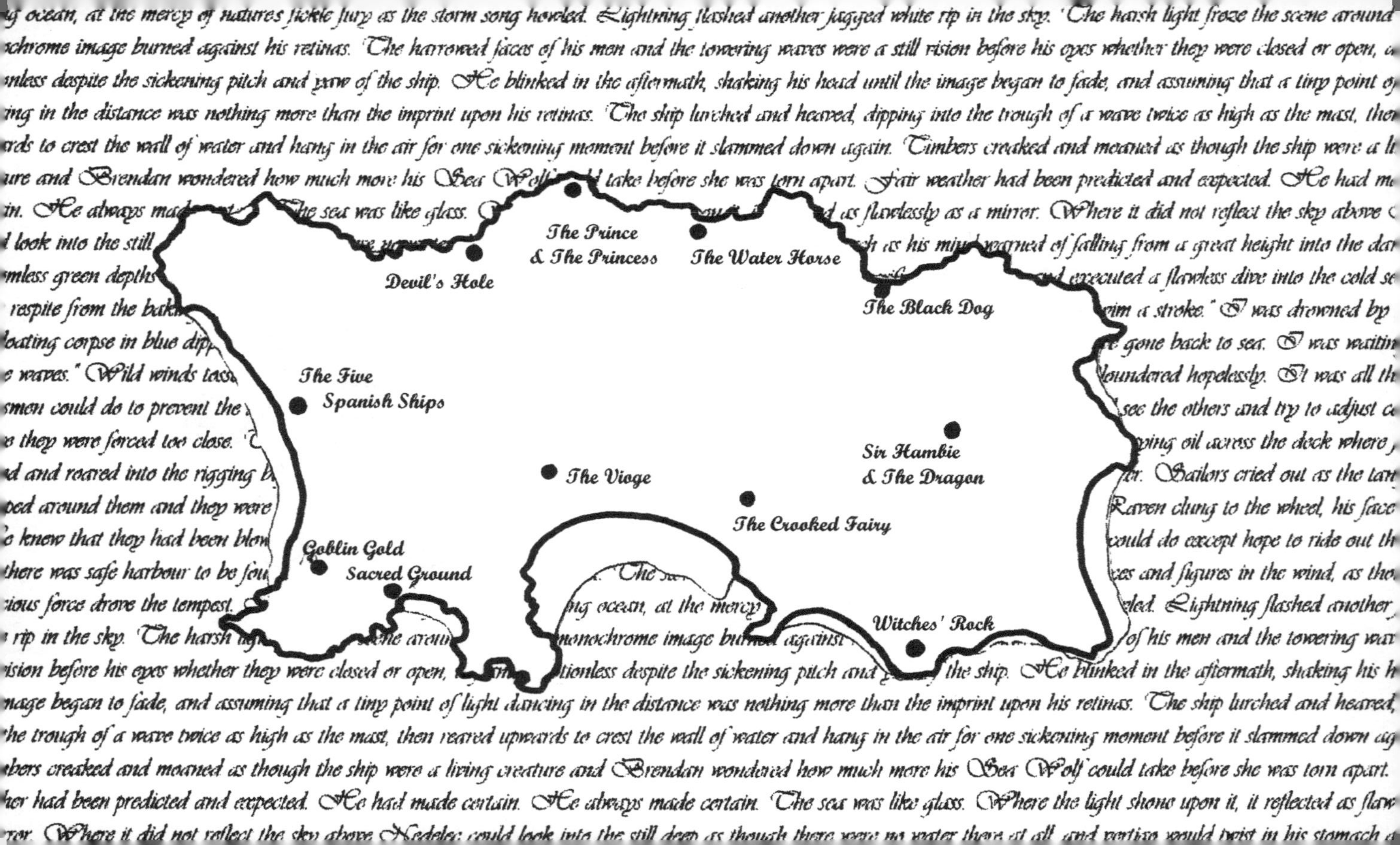

The Five

Spanish Ships

Goblin Gold

Sacred Ground

Devil's Hole

The Prince
& The Princess

The Water Horse

The Visage

The Black Dog

The Crooked Fairy

Sir Humbie
& The Dragon

Witches' Rock

Acknowledgements

There are a handful of people without whom the writing of this book would have been a far more difficult process.

I owe my gratitude first and foremost to my mother, for all her help and support as well as her patient re-readings and timely snack-feedings. A huge thank you to the friends, near and far, who provided critical readings of the text: Lizzie Martin, writer Cody McCloud and novelist Noah Goats for their feedback and encouragement, and Charlotte Le Sauteur for the combination of proofreading and physiotherapy.

My thanks to writer Jeremy Harrison, who as well as providing illustrations for the book gave such helpful notes on the stories, to Naomi Irene Rohatyn, my comedy-writing partner for all her support and enthusiasm, and to Rachelle Mandik for her invaluable advice.

A special tip of the hat to my eagle-eyed draft editor James Hovey for the generosity with which he provided his valuable experience and time.

My thanks as well to all of the wonderful schoolteachers who guided my reading and encouraged my writing, especially Mrs Sheila Jenkins, Mrs Poole, Mrs Heath, Mr Leon Shaw, and the late Mr Herbert.

I am enormously grateful to Nicola Guy at The History Press, not only for her help and guidance, but for taking a chance on a new author, and I am most indebted to my project editor Ruth Boyes for all of her kindness, patience and hard work in refining the text.

INTRODUCTION

Jersey was the land of the fairies
and the race is yet believed to exist.

S.J. Coleman, *Treasury of Folklore*

Every place has its own unique mythological stories, carved and created as much by the landscape in which they are set as by the people who once inhabited those places.

The island of Jersey is a singular place of great natural beauty which lends itself well to fairy tales. The dramatic cliffs of the north coast are as beautiful in their rugged majesty as the sand dunes of the western shores and the golden beaches that surround the island. Jersey's patchwork of green farmland is interspersed with rich woodland, and medieval castles are juxtaposed with the bustling hub of the town. Jersey is home to one of the world's busiest offshore finance centres and has a population of almost 100,000 people.

Like a threadbare tapestry, the whole picture of Jersey's vibrant mythology is hard to make out. Many tales of the monsters and mysteries of the island have been worn down by time to bare descriptions and the locations in which they took place. Some tales are comical, others are tragic, and a few of the legends chill the blood. Disparate sources make veiled references to the notion that Jersey was the chosen final refuge of the fairy race. There are even dark reports of fairies so distressed by the impact of human colonisation and industrialisation that they hanged themselves from the ancient stone dolmens. Winding through much of the folklore are brief mentions of the mysterious and anonymous White Lady and her association with the many dolmens and standing stones upon the island. There are even allusions to doorways between worlds.

The antics of many supernatural creatures have not been recorded, or perhaps were never told as complete stories. They may only have been constructed as vague warnings designed to keep children away from certain dangerous areas like clifftops and dark woods or out of the savage sea currents. No doubt many tales are irretrievably lost to the passage of time, since the surviving legends are ancient. Most travelled down the centuries by oral tradition, changing through the ages like a complex game of Chinese whispers lasting a thousand years or more.

Often the recorded details of each local legend vary greatly from report to report, evolving drastically or altering thematically depending upon the periods in which they were written. Perhaps it is not surprising then that so many of these rich and varied fairy tales have been lost in translation and forgotten over time.

At only forty-five square miles in size, Jersey is the largest, as well as the most southerly, of the British Channel Isles. The islands are located in the bay of Mont St Michel and on any clear day it is possible to stand on the coast of Jersey and see the beaches of France quite plainly with the naked eye.

It is estimated that Jersey became an island around 8000 BC. During very low tides it is still possible to see the remains of the great forest, now fossilised, upon the land that once joined Jersey to the main body of France. In what is now the bay of St Ouen the hoof prints of a deer remain in the petrified earth where it walked millennia ago.

The ancient history of Jersey is a violent one. The people of the island were beset by pirates and Vikings in the early centuries and then became victims to the continual power struggle between the French and the English for ownership of the Channel Islands.

The island's most beautiful fortifications, the huge castle of Mont Orgueil in the north-east and Elizabeth Castle in the south, are testament to the centuries of war that the island endured.

Conflict came again to the Channel Islands when they fell under Nazi occupation between 1940 and 1945 during the Second World War. The island is scarred with German fortifications from these years. Gun mountings and bunkers litter the high points of the island, grim and incongruous reminders of some of the island's darkest years, set against the glorious backdrop of the coastline.

Jersey is now an English-speaking island, but until very recent times the people of Jersey were French-speaking and the French that they spoke was the dialectal Jèrraise, now understood only by a dwindling few. From the year 1820 onwards an influx of English speakers began to outweigh those using the island's native language and it is estimated that currently only 20 per cent of Jersey residents still have any fluency in Jèrraise at all.

With such a turbulent history, and the loss of its native language, it is understandable that the legends of Jersey are relatively unknown by the present generation of islanders.

My own interest in the fairy tales of Jersey began when I started work on a fantasy novel set within the island. I had an idea that I wanted to incorporate some local legends into the story and I began to research the folklore of the island. I was astounded at the depth and complexity of the mythology, as well as the sheer variety of fairy creatures rumoured to have inhabited the island. The north coast in particular is so populated with legends it seems unlikely that any humble resident in ancient Jersey could have expected to leave their home of an evening without encountering at least one supernatural creature.

Bouley Bay's Black Dog has a certain notoriety, I suspect, due to the beautiful old country tavern of the same name which has stood for centuries by the bay. Certain stories, such as the tale of Sir Hambie's battle with the dragon, and that of Madelaine's confrontation with the witches of Rocqueberg, are recorded only in synoptic descriptions.

While the famous kelpie of Bonne Nuit Bay is a staple of Celtic folklore, and is well known compared to the other fairy tales, some of the more obscure local legends, like that of the Vioge and the Crooked Fairy, appear to have no archetypal ancestors in any other national mythology and are unique to Jersey alone.

With such vibrant and intriguing heroes and monsters slowly fading as they are consumed by the past, it is important that these stories be retold. Definitive versions of the tales have been difficult to capture, since they have either altered and evolved through centuries of oral tradition, or been almost forgotten entirely. Some had been presented in so many forms that the essence of the legends were distorted as though by a hall of mirrors. Others were as thin as ghosts, haunting the footnotes of old or academic texts, and remembered only in the localities that are named after them.

This collection of the legends of Jersey is an attempt to carry the rich and complex characters of Jersey's ancient mythology into the modern day, fully realised in complete stories, so that their place in the history of the island is not forgotten by Jersey's people and lost to history.

Sir Hambie and the Dragon

The dragon flew into Jersey ahead of a storm, seeking refuge from the driving wind and rain. She intended only to take shelter from the elements, but soon found the richly fatted cattle of the little island to her taste. Finding no resistance from the scattered and terrified rural community, she made her den in the marshes of St Lawrence and decided to stay.

She was a young green dragon, only seven centuries old, with a hide like leather and scales the colour of wet jade. While she was not as immense as the great dragons of old, she was large and powerful enough that she did not need to fear any other living creature upon the island.

She wreaked havoc upon the meagre population, hunting and burning at will. The desperation of the people of Jersey soon began to outstrip their fear of the creature, and a group of men ventured into the marshes intending to slay the dragon. One man had lost his young son to it. Another had seen his wife taken by it. There was a farmer who had watched his herd of dairy cows torn apart by the creature for no more reason than its love of cruelty. They were accompanied by a few young men determined to prove themselves as heroes. Taking what weapons they had, they walked into the misty reaches of the dragon's lair to do battle.

None of them returned.

News of the dragon spread fast and wide, carried by the fleeing islanders, and soon came to the ears of a young knight in Normandy named Sir Michael of Hambie, who resolved at once to travel to Jersey and destroy the creature.

He had but one task to complete first. With slightly more trepidation than he felt about facing the dragon, Sir Michael sought out his wife to inform her of his decision.

He found Elise in the stables feeding slices of apple to his white warhorse, Lexen. The stallion was nibbling them daintily from her open palm. Sir Michael's grey eyes softened as he watched her. Elise was nearly as tall and fair as he was himself, and the earnest manner in which she was whispering to his horse made him smile.

'Elise,' Michael's crisp voice made his wife spin, with a guilty grin, to face him, 'you'll make him fat if you keep spoiling him. I can't go into battle on a fat warhorse.'

Elise laughed, 'Oh, you know I can't help it,' she shrugged, 'he's just so sweet.'

Lexen whickered and nudged Lady Hambie gently, his attention upon the remaining apple in her hands.

'You should be ashamed of yourself,' Michael told the stallion with mock severity as he strode forward to scratch the horse's forelock and help feed him the last of the apple. 'Stuffing your greedy face when we have important things to do.'

'Important things?' The smile slipped from Elise's lips and her dark eyes searched Michaels's face carefully. 'What do you mean?'

Michael slid a hand around Elise's waist and drew her close as he began, 'There is a dragon in the island of Jersey and—'

'No,' Elise interrupted firmly, placing a hand upon his chest. 'No. You're not going.' She stared at him incredulously, shaking her head. 'A dragon, Michael? A giant fire-breathing monster the size of a barn? You cannot seriously mean to fight such a thing.'

She tried to remove herself from his embrace, but her stern dignity was compromised slightly by a tangle of hay in her golden hair. Michael smiled as he pulled her against him.

'Elise,' he reasoned, 'what sort of a knight would I be if I did not do my utmost to protect the people of that island? I have sworn oaths to defend the innocent. Besides,' he tilted his head and added, his eyes sparkling, 'how many men ever get the chance to slay a dragon?'

'Michael!' Elise stamped her foot in annoyance. 'It would be wiser to raise an army against the thing than fight it alone. Why must you always be the hero?' She ceased struggling against his embrace and wrapped her arms around him tightly. 'And what would I do if you were killed?'

Sir Michael tilted Elise's chin up with one hand, forcing her to meet his gaze, and kissed her with infinite tenderness.

'It would take more than one little dragon to stop me from coming back to you,' he said quietly, 'and there is no time to raise an army.'

'I hate you,' Elise said, burying her face against his neck as she clung to him.

'Yes, I can see that,' Michael smiled as he picked the hay out of her curls with his slender fingers and let it fall to the floor.

'I suppose you think that you'll be taking Lexen on this fool's errand?' she demanded.

'I do, yes,' Michael said, 'because he is my horse, and if I have to walk around in full plate armour all day searching for a dragon, I shall simply fall over when I find it.'

'This isn't funny, Michael!' Elise took his face in her hands and looked at him beseechingly. 'Please don't go. There must be someone else who can slay the thing?'

'It's killing people, Elise,' Michael's grey eyes became serious. 'I have to go. There is no one else.'

The white stallion whickered and flattened his ears.

Michael felt Elise startle in his arms as her eyes focused behind him, and he turned to follow her gaze.

'Ah, Francis,' he said in surprise as he spotted his young squire waiting in the shadows, 'how long have you been there? I shall need you to polish my armour and sharpen my sword. We sail with the next tide for the Isle of Jersey. They have a dragon that needs to be dealt with.'

'Good God, Francis, why must you always be lurking?' Elise asked, clearly annoyed. 'Not that it matters. You won't have time to break the habit, since my husband has gone insane and you will both be dead by this time tomorrow.'

The squire's eyes widened and he grimaced as he smoothed his dark hair down nervously.

'A dragon, my Lord? That sounds very dangerous.'

'You are the most pigeon-hearted lad I ever knew, Francis,' the knight said affectionately. 'This is a chance to fight a dragon. To save lives! Legends are made of such things. Make ready, boy. There is no time to lose.'

'Yes, my Lord,' Francis said quietly, 'if those are your orders, my Lord.'

'It's just one dragon, Elise,' Michael added after the squire had left, 'and they say it's just a green. No bigger than a haystack really.'

'Oh well, as long as it's only a small dragon,' Elise said sarcastically, 'then I shan't worry at all. Why did I marry a raving lunatic?'

Sir Michael tilted his head thoughtfully, 'I *think* you said it was because you loved me so much that you found it hard to breathe.'

'I had probably had too much wine when I said that,' Elise responded tartly, but a smile quivered across her lips.

'Don't be angry at me, my love.' The knight took her hands gently, 'You know I have to help those people. It is who I am.'

Elise realised then that his resolve would not be swayed and begged, 'At least take Brion and his men with you. Francis is worse than useless.'

Michael shook his head firmly, 'The Captain of the Guard stays here at Castle Hambie with you. Your safety is more important to me than anything else, you know that. Just let me go now, Elise, and I will return to you as soon as I can.'

Elise clenched her fists and choked back bitter words, then nodded and allowed her husband to prepare.

He departed the next day with her grudging blessing. She waved his ship away from the harbour tearfully, standing upon the dock until he was entirely lost to view in the morning mist.

Sir Michael's squire was violently ill on the passage to Jersey and the knight could not help but be slightly amused as he carefully moved his white cloak away from his wretched servant.

'Poor Francis,' he said, 'I'm not entirely sure you should have been a squire. You don't seem all that suited to a life of adventure.'

'Never really had the stomach for adventure,' the squire responded weakly.

'I can see that,' said Sir Michael with a grin.

The squire regarded the slender, blonde Lord of Hambie resentfully for a long moment before leaning back over the rail and retching loudly.

Even before the ship was fully ashore Sir Michael mounted his horse and urged Lexen into the sea. The powerful white charger leapt into the shallows and churned surf as horse and rider galloped up the beach. Once Francis was ashore and awkwardly mounted onto his own horse, the two men made their way inland and north towards the marsh of St Lawrence where the dragon was rumoured to dwell.

They rode on late into the night, searching the marshland, wet and exhausted, calling out to anyone they saw, but nobody had seen the beast. Though it grew late and they grew weary, Sir Michael would not waiver.

Deep into the night they spotted a glow to the east.

'That isn't the dawn,' Michael mused aloud, 'that's fire. Maybe even dragon fire. Whether it is or not, there may still be people who need help.'

The flames were distant, however. By the time they reached the source, which was a barn aflame, there was little left save for a burned-out shell. The dying embers illuminated two young children huddled together, a girl and boy soot-stained and pale with horror.

'It killed my father,' the young boy told Sir Michael. His face was dotted with blood, 'It killed him right in front of me. Then it dragged our mule into the woods. I hid,' he admitted on a sob, 'I just hid with my sister and I didn't even try to stop it.'

The knight dismounted and knelt before the boy to lay a hand on his shoulder.

'You did right to hide,' Michael told him. 'You survived, and there is no shame in that. Your father would want you to protect your family and grow into a man. I will avenge him, if I can. Which way did it go, boy?'

The boy pointed a shaking finger toward the dark woods and Michael swiftly remounted and swung Lexen around.

'Let us wait for daylight,' Francis said, 'it could be anywhere in there.'

'No,' Michael fitted his helmet onto his head, the visor raised, 'the damned thing might be gone if we wait, and I'll not have another death on my conscience if it kills again while we sit here like children afraid of the dark. Besides, every minute we wait is another minute for Elise to fret. We ride now.'

'You ride on if you wish,' Francis said quietly, 'I'll not go into those woods.'

Sir Michael regarded his squire with something like pity for a long moment, then turned away. He urged Lexen on with his heels and rode alone into the darkness.

He picked his way with care, stopping often, listening intently. Even in the weak moonlight the dragon was not hard to track. It left a trail of broken branches hanging from the trees. There was a sulphurous scent, and gouges in the earth where its claws had torn the ground. Lexen snorted at the dragon's smell but did not hesitate or falter, his iron-shod hooves quiet on the soft ground.

Dawn had touched the trees with a cold glow by the time Sir Michael entered a clearing and found the creature. The dragon was sleeping next to the remains of a torn animal carcass. The hapless mule taken from the farm, Michael presumed.

The knight looked on in awe as the dragon's chest rose and fell with each breath. A fine haze of smoke rose from her nostrils.

Michael took a moment to admit to himself that the creature was somewhat larger than he had been expecting. She was curled like a giant cat; her tail wrapped around her body and resting over her muzzle. He could feel Lexen trembling as the warhorse's training and nature battled within him. Instinct told the horse to flee, but Michael knew his steed would stand with him to the death. He dismounted as quietly as he could and removed his silver-inlaid sword and shield from the saddle, wincing at every clink of his armour and glancing repeatedly at the sleeping dragon. He then patted the stallion's neck.

'Go on with you now, boy,' he whispered to the horse, 'I won't see you be a meal for this monster. Elise would never forgive me. Go on!' he repeated giving the stallion a soft slap on the rump.

The warhorse circled him once uncertainly, like a white ghost in the shadows, and then cantered away into the trees.

Sir Michael turned back to the sleeping dragon and approached slowly, drawing his sword. He hesitated, the blade inches from the giant lizard's face. Like a statue carved from emerald, she was beautiful, yet she was terrifying to behold. In this moment she was also utterly defenceless.

The knight poised to strike, and then lowered his sword.

Michael swore under his breath.

'I'm a fool,' he whispered, then took a breath.

'Wake up!' he shouted into the dragon's face, 'I won't kill a sleeping enemy, not even one as vile as you, so *wake up!*'

Green eyes the size of saucers snapped open as Michael slammed the hilt of his sword hard into the bridge of the dragon's nose. The emerald eyes narrowed. The dragon's tail uncurled like a whip, sweeping Michael off of his feet with its barbed tip and hurling him into a bush. The dragon moved towards him without hesitation, lunging at his left leg as Michael kicked out. She roared in fury as his steel-clad heel snapped off one of her fangs. She bit down upon

Michael's shin, crushing the armour and causing the knight to yell in pain, but then she hesitated and tilted her head in confusion over the fact that her prey was clad in an iron hide.

Michael smashed his shield into the dragon's face and it reared back with a snarl and opened its jaws wide. Anticipating her attack, Michael struggled into a crouch and held his shield in front of him as an explosion of flame jetted from between the dragon's jaws and roared around him. The heat was blistering. He had to tear his cloak from his back as the fabric caught fire. He threw the burning cloth into the dragon's face, and she shook her head like a wet dog to cast it away.

Michael stood, took two swift steps forward and swung his sword. The dragon flinched away and the blade opened a shallow wound across her chest. She screamed in pain and fury. The knight swung again but the dragon turned and his blade glanced harmlessly off of the hard scales of her shoulder. An instant later her tail struck him again like a flail as she spun, clubbing him down into the dirt with a force that knocked his helmet rattling into the trees and made his head swim.

Before Michael could begin to get up, a great gust of wind blew dust into his eyes, tossing debris and leaves everywhere. Another gust followed. The dragon was taking to the air, her beating wings bending the branches of trees with their force.

'No you don't,' Michael gasped, struggling to his feet.

As he stood, the dragon's great claws clamped onto his shoulders and he felt his feet leave the ground. Every beat of her wings lifted them a little higher, but the dragon was straining and Michael realised that, with his plate armour, he was heavy prey for his opponent to lift. Still, however slowly, they were beginning to rise and Sir Michael had no wish to be dropped and smashed open like an egg.

He jabbed upwards with his sword and managed to strike a glancing blow off of one of the dragon's legs. They were above the height of a tall man and rising. The knight threw off his shield so that he could grip his sword two-handed and swing it with more force above his head. He caught a lucky slash on the dragon's stomach. Shallow, he judged, but probably painful. He repeated the action and was rewarded for his efforts by a roar as he was dropped from fifteen feet in the air. He landed with a sound like cookware being hurled at a wall.

The impact knocked the air from his lungs and he was barely able to turn onto his back before he was doused in a gout of flame. Michael threw his arms across his face and rolled as best he could under cover, wrinkling his nose at the smell of his burnt hair. Another intense burst of flame erupted and ignited the bushes around him. He could feel his armour starting to heat up. Spying his shield, he turned over to crawl towards it. The dragon pounced, slamming her full weight down upon him with a ringing clang, driving his face into the dirt. Without his armour Michael would have been crushed in an instant. He could not move or breathe. The dragon stamped and Michael groaned as he felt a rib snap. Despite the hollow bones that made her light enough to fly, the dragon's weight still felt immense.

The dragon slowly curved her sinuous neck low to the ground so that she was looking into Michael's eyes. The cold intelligence in her rich green gaze chilled him to the bone. She had won and she knew it.

She flexed her claws against his armoured backplate curiously and the metal shrieked as she ran an exploratory claw to where his breastplate met his shoulder guard. Finding the gap between them she reached her claw inside and pushed it into the flesh under his arm.

Michael heard himself trying to cry out without air in his lungs. The pain was overwhelming, terrifying, he couldn't breathe, his body convulsed. His vision began to blur and the ringing in his ears almost prevented him from hearing a sound like thunder, drawing nearer, drumming, like the sound of galloping, like …

Lexen reared and slammed his front hooves, iron-shod and sharpened for battle, into the face of the dragon.

The weight upon Michael shifted as the dragon recoiled, and air, sweet, blessed air, filled his lungs as he rolled onto his back. The dragon clawed at a ruined eye, blood pouring down her face. She thrashed in agony. Her barbed tail missed the stallion by an inch as Lexen leapt. The horse twisted and kicked out with his hind legs, striking hard into her chest. The dragon stumbled and fought not to fall as the stallion bucked and lashed at her, then she opened her maw and spat flames blindly at the white horse.

Lexen's mane blazed and the instinctive fear of fire forced the stallion back. He whinnied piteously as he stood over his master, his forelock reduced to smouldering stubble.

'Go!' Michael gasped, 'Good boy, Lexen, but go now,' the knight forced himself to his feet, feeling blood trickling down his side, draining his strength as he gripped his sword. He strode forward through the fire. The dragon's ruined eye blinded her to his approach. He swung, clumsily but with desperate strength, hacking the blade into her neck.

Claws tore at his armour, shaking him like a rag doll as he shifted his weight and struck again. Flames exploded around him and he turned his head as he swung again wildly, his arms jarring with contact as the sword slammed this time against harder scales. She whipped her tail at him, but Michael was expecting it and cut hard and low with his sword. The blade sliced cleanly through the narrowest point of her tail, severing the barb at its tip. She writhed and roared, striking him with her neck. They fell together, the dragon onto her side and Michael to his knees. He aimed a blow at her chest, missing as the dragon convulsed, spewing fire. Heedless of her flames, slicing claws and snapping teeth, Michael brought his sword up with grim determination and hacked into the scales of her neck again and again, more like a woodsman with a blunt axe than a master swordsman, until her head separated from her body and she fell still. Then Sir Michael's strength gave out and he dropped his sword with a clatter, bowing his head, breathless and trembling.

He remained still until he felt Lexen nibbling fondly at his scorched hair, and stirred as he realised he was still bleeding steadily. The knight struggled to undo the straps on his breastplate, his fingers sore and burned, cursing Francis the squire under his breath for not being nearby to help him. Eventually he managed to work the straps loose and tossed his breastplate away with a clang to carefully examine the wound under his arm. Blood had soaked through his clothing. He stripped his scorched undershirt off awkwardly. The wound did not appear to be as deep as he had feared; certainly not mortal in itself provided he could staunch the flow of blood and avoid infection from the dragon's filthy claws. His burns were painful but not severe enough to give him concern.

Tearing a strip from his discarded shirt, Michael jammed it under his arm and allowed himself a weak grin. Lexen had trotted over to the dragon's corpse and was blowing out through his nostrils in disgust and confusion as the fae creature's body turned slowly to stone.

'Not bad for your first dragon,' Sir Michael told his steed. 'Maybe you can do the next one all by yourself. I'm hurt rather badly but I dare say I'll make it home in one piece. If Elise doesn't kill me, I might live to fight another day. Now, don't think any less of me, Lexen, but I think I'm going to faint,' and so saying, the Lord of Hambie slumped to the ground unconscious.

It was several hours before Francis ventured into the woods to see what had become of his master. He walked the same path of destruction that Sir Michael had followed in the dark hours before dawn, but now the sun was rising in the sky and the passage of the dragon was unmistakable.

On entering the clearing, Francis stopped in awe at the sight of the stone dragon sprawled near its severed head, and then smiled to see his lord laying, apparently dead, beside it.

'Arrogant fool,' Francis whispered.

Walking closer he toed Sir Michael's body and was startled to hear a soft groan emerge from the prone knight. Francis exclaimed in horror and stepped back, staring at Sir Michael's scorched hair, the bloody shirt and the bruises beginning to darken his pale, lean torso.

'Francis?' Michael stirred and winced, opening one grey eye to squint upwards, 'I'm a little wounded I'm afraid. Could you help me please?'

'Of course,' said the squire, composing his features. 'Show me,' he insisted, lifting Michael's arm and dragging away the wadded cloth that concealed the wound beneath.

Michael hissed in pain as his blood began to flow again and then managed a weak grin, his teeth white against his soot-smeared skin.

'How bad does it look?' the knight asked, raising one scorched brow.

'Not as bad as it could be.'

Francis drew his dagger and drove it deep into Sir Michael's wound.

He did not meet Michael's eyes as the knight cried out, but twisted the blade, piercing Michael's heart. He felt the knight's hot blood pour over his hand and marvelled at the ease of what he had done.

Michael shuddered, his hands grasping at Francis's arms.

'But Elise …' he said in confusion.

Then his head fell back and his eyes closed.

'Yes,' Francis whispered, 'Elise.'

There was a brief moment of silence before Lexen's hooves smashed down on Francis's shoulders, battering him to the ground, cutting into his flesh. The squire flailed onto his back, looking up in horror at the warhorse as iron-shod hooves slammed down into his chest like hammers. A hoof glanced off Francis's skull, stunning him as he tried to roll away.

The squire grabbed desperately at Sir Michael's sword and lashed out at the stallion's legs with the blade, opening a line of red against the stark white. Francis screamed at the creature, struggled to his feet, then feinted a lunge. The white horse, used to the squire's petty cruelties, reared back over the body of his fallen master protectively as Francis backed out of the clearing and fled.

⟨૪⟩

Lady Hambie had not been able to sleep or eat while her husband was gone, and had spent most of her time in the highest tower of Castle Hambie, straining her eyes towards the barely visible coast of Jersey in the hope of seeing Michael's ship return. She had taken a brief respite to lay down in exhaustion when her lady-in-waiting arrived breathless, to tell her that a boat was pulling into the harbour flying Sir Michael's colours. Elise made her way, in a flurry of long skirts, down the steps of the tower and ran to the dock, her hair streaming out like a golden pennant, leaving her maid panting in her wake.

The Captain of the Guard and several of his men raced along behind her at a barely respectful distance, arriving in a thunder of boots upon the wooden dock with a force that made it vibrate violently.

'Do you see him, Captain Brion?' Elise demanded, 'Oh, why don't they hurry?'

As the ship drew up slowly to the dock, Elise cried out, 'Where is Michael? Where is my husband? If he is hiding to provoke me,' Elise added to Captain Brion with a laughing sob, 'I shall push him into the water and hope he sinks like a rock in his stupid armour.'

Seeing Francis at the rail of the boat, Elise called again, 'Where is Sir Michael?'

'The Lord of Hambie is dead, my lady Elise,' the squire said as he stepped unsteadily onto the dock. 'He was killed by the dragon.'

'No,' the word was an exhalation.

Elise crumpled, collapsing into the folds of her skirts, unable to breathe. She put one hand to her throat and one to her bodice as she struggled to draw air into her lungs.

'No,' she gasped, 'it is a trick. He thinks to surprise me and laugh at my fear. Say that it is a trick!'

'Is it true?' Captain Brion demanded of Francis as he knelt beside Lady Hambie. 'Speak, you fool!'

'The dragon killed Sir Michael,' Francis said. 'There was a great battle and both were gravely wounded. I triumphed at last by cutting off the monster's head, but Sir Michael suffered a mortal injury.' Francis squared his narrow shoulders, 'I killed the dragon and made it to Sir Michael's side in time to hear his final wishes.'

Francis hesitated and licked his lips nervously, smoothing down his dark hair.

'He was crushed beneath the creature, so I could not return his body. However, it was Sir Michael's wish and his command, that as reward for my service and my … my bravery in slaying the dragon … I am to inherit his lands and titles and take Lady Hambie as my wife. This was his wish and his command to us all.'

Elise crawled quietly to the edge of the dock and vomited into the water.

The wedding between Francis and Elise was not a joyful event. Elise had seemed to sleepwalk through the ceremony, her cheeks wet with tears. She had spoken barely a word since the news of her husband's death had reached her ears. She had only asked what had become of her husband's horse. She had received the answer from Francis that Lexen had thrown his rider before being killed by the dragon.

Captain Brion had stayed close by Elise during the feast, his hand resting protectively on her forearm in the hope that he could offer some small measure of comfort. The squire, for Brion could not think of Francis as anything else, laughed too loudly and drank too much beside his fragile wife. Brion realised that he had been hoping Lady Hambie would rouse from her bereaved stupor long enough to order Brion to run the squire through for his damned impudence in presuming to

her hand, regardless of any dying wishes Sir Michael may have had. His Lord must have been near death and delirious indeed to think such a match anything beyond madness. The squire had not even allowed Lady Hambie a period of mourning, no doubt afraid that Elise would refuse him once she was not utterly numb with grief.

As Brion watched, Francis drew Elise away from the grim marriage party and up the stairs towards his master's old bedchamber. The Captain of the Guard had to grit his teeth against calling out to Elise, and instead followed at a discreet distance.

Elise walked slowly up the stairs to the chambers that she had shared with her first husband, ignoring the man who walked eagerly ahead of her. The squire was a shadow compared to her Michael, and she was utterly indifferent to him.

'I did as you wished, my love,' she murmured to her husband's memory, 'I married the squire, but I cannot live this way.'

'What's that, Elise, my darling?' Francis enquired as he ushered her into the bedchamber.

Elise walked to her bureau as Francis began to undress. He kicked off his boots and staggered drunkenly for a moment. She opened a drawer and drew out a dagger that Michael had commissioned for her on a whim. It was a pretty and ornate piece designed to look like a miniature version of his sword. The same sword that Francis was currently unbuckling from his waist and allowing to drop with a clatter to the floor.

Elise placed the tip of the dagger at her throat and felt a peace descend upon her as she drew in a last breath. She turned to offer a farewell to her husband's squire, who was looking at her in a horror of realisation. Elise's lips parted to speak and then remained open in surprise as she looked at the squire's bared chest. Her eyes darkened and she lowered the dagger even as her grip upon it tightened.

'Would you care to explain to me, Francis,' Elise said in a voice so soft that the squire could barely hear it, 'why it is that you have hoof-prints upon your chest?'

Francis looked down stupidly.

'Oh that. Yes. The horse kicked me as it was trying to run away.'

'Really,' Elise's grip on the dagger became so tight that her hand began to tremble. 'If Lexen *kicked* you, the hoof-prints would be upside down, would they not?'

'The heat of battle,' Francis protested vaguely. 'He reared up at me perhaps. You have no idea what it's like or how a man's memories may be affected by the trauma of ...'

'Turn around that I may see the rest of you,' Lady Elise commanded imperiously. 'Is there a single mark from a dragon's claw? A single burn from dragon fire? Show me!'

Francis began to reach for his shirt, 'I am your husband now,' he said as sternly as he could manage, 'and you shall treat me with respect, or I shall discipline you as I see fit.'

Elise gave a humourless snort of laughter as he moved towards her.

'Tell me, Francis,' she spat, 'how is it exactly that a valiant knight like my husband was killed, and a snivelling cur like you lived?'

Francis's face distorted with rage and he snarled, 'Because I killed him! Because he was an entitled, arrogant fool who deserved to die for his idiocy, and if you are so bent on joining him then I can assist you!'

'Guards!' Elise screamed.

Captain Brion burst through the door with such force that the lower hinge snapped.

He found Lady Hambie struggling with Francis and, with great pleasure, lifted the squire off of his feet and slammed him face first into the floor.

'He killed Michael,' Elise sobbed, as Francis struggled on the ground. 'See where Lexen tried to defend my husband? The squire's wounds betray him!'

'She's mad with grief,' Francis shouted. 'She speaks nonsense! I am your master now and you will unhand me!'

Captain Brion gripped Francis by the throat and dragged him to the door.

'What would you have me do with him, Lady Hambie?' Brion asked, tightening his grip on Francis's throat so that the man could not protest again.

'Gather those guests who have not already departed, and find some rope,' Lady Hambie smiled coldly as she wiped her tears. 'We shall have a hanging this night.'

☙❧

Lady Hambie and her Captain of the Guard sailed with the next morning's tide. It did not take them long to find the place where Sir Michael had been murdered by the squire who claimed to have killed the dragon. The island was alive with the news of the monster's demise.

A few shy people greeted them as they neared the place where its body lay, and the boy that Sir Michael had spoken to before he went into battle stepped forward bravely.

'We all knew that the squire had not killed the dragon, my Lady,' the farm boy said deferentially as he led them into the woods. 'We could hear the battle raging as dawn broke and then hours later that squire walks into the forest, walks out again not but ten minutes later claiming *he's* killed the dragon. I told my mum, I said "Mum, you might as well tell people *you* killed the dragon and it'd be as likely a story," that's what I said, my Lady.'

'Are we near?' Elise enquired.

'Almost there, Lady Hambie,' the boy said as they walked down the now well-worn path. 'We would have moved Sir Michael's body and given him a proper burial, only we couldn't my Lady, so we raised a cairn over him and people have been laying stones and flowers there.'

'Why could you not move him?' Elise asked.

'On account of the white horse, Lady Hambie,' the boy explained. 'He won't be moved, and while he's as gentle as a lamb most of the time, he fights like a demon when anyone tries to lead him off.'

'Lexen!' Elise cried as she broke into the clearing and saw her husband's stallion. The white horse gave a shrill whinny of recognition and trotted to her, pressing his face into her chest. He had a bandage about his foreleg and had been stripped of his armour and brushed, with his burns tended to. All around them people were gathered to pay their respects, and they gazed with curiosity at their saviour's wife.

'I've been taking care of him,' the farm boy added proudly, patting the stallion affectionately, 'it seemed the least I could do. He likes apples.'

'Oh yes, he certainly does. You have my thanks,' Elise whispered, wrapping her fingers in the singed remains of Lexen's mane. 'You have my eternal thanks.'

The cairn of stones was raised higher than a man, as though each person who had come to pay their respects had added to the monument, but the stones were barely visible beneath the veil of flowers that covered them. Elise stared at the stone remains of the dragon, horrified at the size, before she knelt beside her husband's makeshift grave.

The day grew long and night crept in before the Captain of the Guard at last placed his hand softly upon Elise's shoulder.

'Let us take Lexen home, my Lady. There is nothing but sorrow for us here.'

'Leave my husband's grave, Brion?' Elise shook her head and wiped her eyes. 'How can I go home where I will not even be able to visit the place that he is buried?'

And the people of Jersey heard and they built the cairn higher, and higher, into a great hill of stone and earth which covered both Sir Michael of Hambie and the dragon that he had slain for them, until it rose like a tor from the landscape. They named it La Hougue Hambie, and on a clear day Lady Hambie could look out from the highest tower of her home in Normandy and see the place where Sir Michael was forever remembered.

It still stands to this day.

THE BLACK DOG OF BOULEY BAY

On nights when the black dog roamed the hills of Bouley Bay, people would lock themselves in their houses, bar the shutters and bolt their doors. Those who had glimpsed the black dog gave varying reports of what it looked like. Some said it was the size of a bull, smooth-furred with ears flat like a hound and huge eyes as yellow as gold. Others swore that the black dog was similar to a great black wolf the size of a bear, with eyes that glowed as red as the flames of hell.

Many insisted that a sighting of the legendary black dog heralded a coming storm or the death of a loved one, while some said that he led lost travellers to safety. Others warned that the black dog chased unwary folk to their deaths from the cliffs, or that he savaged people viciously. Some people swore that the black dog would protect the vulnerable from harm.

Whether the black dog was an evil spirit or some benevolent freak of nature was a topic of much debate in the area. Sceptics muttered that the whole thing was a rumour spread by smugglers to keep people away from the area at night, but when the eerie howls echoed down into the bay, anyone who heard them would make for the nearest house or for The Black Dog tavern just to be on the safe side.

It was a night late in May, and sea mist hung heavy on the hillsides, when the locals heard a ghostly howl echoing across the bay and locked themselves safely away once again. On this particular night, any who had glimpsed the black dog might have wondered why it appeared so clumsy. They might have considered, had they hesitated to observe, that the black dog on this evening was about the size of a pantomime horse, with a large fluffy tail that looked like it was made from feathers and wired onto its body. The black dog moved with a slow, irregular gait, and at one point, when the back half of it slipped and fell on some wet leaves, it could be heard to curse softly.

Had anyone chosen to follow the erratic path of the black dog down the steep slope to the shore, they might have seen that, as it crunched onto the pebbles and drew near to the water, its rear end stood up and said firmly, 'Right, that's it, Pierre, I'm sick of looking at your backside. I want to be the head on the way back up.'

'Shh!' said Pierre severely. 'Do you realise what will happen if we get caught by the customs men? Keep it down John, for goodness' sake.'

Removing the huge black dog mask from his head, Pierre wiped the sweat from his brow, reached inside the shaggy outfit and rummaged in various internal pockets until he located his pipe. He grasped it in a large, fake paw and lit it with some difficulty.

'Anyway,' Pierre added as he puffed a glow from the pipe, 'I do the howl much better than you, so it makes sense that I be the head.'

'Oh *fine*. Can you see them yet?' John asked, looking out over the waves.

'Can't tell in this fog. They're always late anyway.'

The pair squinted into the mist, listening to gentle waves wash onto the stony beach until a glittering reflection on the water revealed itself as a hooded lantern on the prow of a boat rowing quietly into shore.

'Give us a howl, boys,' chuckled one of the sailors jumping into the shallows.

He crunched pebbles underfoot as he hauled the boat onto land. His two fellows jumped out and the small boat was swiftly unloaded of its small cargo: three kegs of brandy and a bottle of the finest gin.

'Good evening, you vile band of smugglers,' John shook hands with each of the smiling men, while Pierre examined their cargo.

'You've tapped this one,' Pierre said indicating an open keg with his pipe, 'how much of it have you had?'

'Just a sip … just a *few* sips,' said one of the sailors with a wink and a nonchalant wave of his hand as they began preparing to shove the boat back into the water. 'A little to keep the cold away.'

'You know Martin will take this out of your payment, don't you?' John said.

'He always does,' grumbled one of the other men and then, with a grind of shingle and the thumping of boots landing back in the boat, they were disappearing into the fog once again.

'Bloody smugglers,' Pierre muttered after them.

'Three kegs,' John said, weighing one of them in his arms with a grimace, 'this is going to be awkward to carry, especially dressed as half a dog. Couldn't we–'

'No,' said Pierre firmly, 'back in the dog, John. We can't afford to be caught and we have to be home before dawn. It's a hell of a slog up that hill.'

'A monstrous climb,' John agreed with a sigh.

'It's steep and no mistake,' Pierre puffed on his pipe speculatively.

'Almost seems like it might be worth fortifying ourselves with a quick mouthful before we get started,' John mused.

'It couldn't hurt,' Pierre said and from somewhere in the depths of his shaggy chest, he produced a small, battered tin cup and filled it from the tapped keg.

It was, they decided, a very small cup, and so it made sense to fill it a couple of times and drink down the contents with gusto before they eventually stowed the bottle of gin in John's trousers. They hung the open keg around Pierre's neck as though he were a St Bernard, took a sealed keg each to carry inside of the dog suit, and began the slow ascent from the bay.

'You came well prepared, Pierre,' John said as they trudged slowly back up the hill.

'You don't know the half of it, John,' Pierre said, 'I've got two pies in my pack in case we get peckish.'

'Now that's thinking ahead!' John said in admiration, 'I thought you smelled appetising this evening. With a long hard climb like this, we're bound to need some sustenance.'

Pierre stopped walking suddenly and John head-butted him lightly in the rear.

'Did you hear that?' Pierre whispered.

'Can't hear much of anything back here, Pierre.'

'Hush!'

'What is it?

'Hush, John.'

John was silent, but after a few moments couldn't resist asking, 'It's not the black dog of Bouley Bay is it? Because he might think we were taking some liberties dressed this way and–'

'Quiet, John! Quick, into the bushes.'

John found himself hauled into a tangle of gorse, and swore softly as he shielded his face against the thorns. He was glad of the thick costume for the first time, as it saved him from the worst of the scratches.

Freeing his head from the dog costume, John could make out the faint sound of low voices carrying through the fog. The mist caused them to seem muffled. The millions of tiny water droplets hampered the sounds and caused the light of a lamp to spread a ghostly glow all around.

'Is it the customs men?' he whispered.

'Be still, John,' Pierre said softly.

They lay in the dark, listening to the muffled voices of men far enough away that they could not tell how many, but close enough to make the hairs rise on the backs of their necks. The illumination faded and the quiet chatter turned to silence, but still John and Pierre waited until they were certain that the men had moved on.

'Do you think they were looking for us?' Pierre asked quietly.

'Very possibly,' John said softly, 'I'm glad I'm quite drunk. I got a bit scared there, Pierre. We nearly had to wash my half of the dog.'

Pierre laughed uneasily as he crawled from the gorse.

'Let's be getting on then,' he said, readjusting his costume.

They struggled up, moving into the darkness beneath the trees. After ten minutes of hard uphill climb they were both breathless and in need of a rest.

'Let's have another cup, Pierre,' John panted, 'whatever we drink will make that thing lighter around your neck.'

'Very thoughtful of you, John,' Pierre agreed, and they stopped to have another drink each.

'I thought I might try my howl again,' John said draining the small cup, 'I've been practising in the bath and I think I might have cracked it.'

'Go ahead,' Pierre said reaching for the little cup, 'the customs men are probably miles away by now. I'll get the pies out so that I'm not looking at you. I wouldn't want you to get stage fright.'

'That's good of you, Pierre,' John cleared his throat with all the solemnity of an opera singer and, inhaling deeply to fill his lungs, he lifted his chin and let out a loud and ghostly howl which echoed and hung in the thick fog.

'Oh yes, that's much better than last time,' Pierre said, impressed. 'Very eerie, very mournful. Here, wet your whistle and have a bite of pie to soothe your throat.'

'Thank you, Pierre,' said John, a little embarrassed, 'it's still not as good a howl as yours though.'

'I try to make mine as low and deep as possible,' said Pierre conspiratorially, before taking a bite of his own squashed pie. 'That way it sounds as though the howl belongs to a very big dog indeed,' he added with his mouth full.

John nodded appreciatively and nibbled delicately on his pie as Pierre wolfed his down.

'If I may?' said Pierre.

'Please do!' John handed him back the cup so that Pierre could wash down his food before clearing his throat and performing an impressive howl.

The sound rang around the bay and John could imagine the residents of the area dipping their heads under their covers or checking the bolts on their doors. The customs officers would have to be brave indeed to risk continuing their search with such a convincing black dog abroad.

'That's so loud, Pierre. I'm going to try again and see if I can do better.'

'Practice makes perfect,' Pierre clapped him on the shoulder and stood up, 'I need to go and, er, water a tree though ...' and with that he stepped away into the shadows to relieve himself.

John howled again, but could match neither the volume nor the depth of Pierre's attempt, so he ended his effort with a disappointed grunt and a sigh. He took a bite of his pie, savouring the flavour.

From the shadows nearby sounded another chilling howl, a sound so primal and so terrifying that hairs stood up on John's neck and arms.

'That was excellent, Pierre,' whispered John in awe. 'You see, that's why you're the master and I am but the apprentice. That's why you're the head. That's why–'

'It wasn't me!' said Pierre reappearing swiftly with his dog's head skewed to one side, hastily doing up his trousers, 'That wasn't me John.'

John reached slowly for the open keg of brandy.

There was the crack of a twig and then, through the fog, they could make out a deeper darkness. A huge shadow detached itself from the trees ahead.

Pierre froze. The small keg dropped from John's numb fingers and rolled downhill unremarked, spilling rich brandy into the soil before coming to rest against a tree. The cheese pie fell from John's other hand as he slowly backed away.

The black dog emerged from the mist. Tendrils of fog curled away from its face as it stepped into the clearing. It was bigger than any dog either man had ever seen. It was powerfully built, like a great wolf, but with the soft flat ears of a retriever. John had heard that the black dog had eyes of hellfire red, or possibly of sulphurous yellow, but as far as John could tell in the pale moonlight, its eyes were as black as the rest of it.

'Pierre,' John said quietly, 'it's looking at me, Pierre.'

'*Don't ... run ...*' Pierre hissed through gritted teeth.

The dog turned its massive head and stared instead, unblinking, at Pierre.

'Now it's looking at you, Pierre,' John whispered.

'I see that, John,' Pierre said gently, 'I see that very clearly, thank you.'

'Maybe you should take off the dog head,' John said, 'so that he doesn't think that you're another dog and try to fight you.'

Pierre slowly removed his half of the dog costume and let it drop to the ground, holding his hands palm up as though in surrender, noticing as he did so that John had bent his knees slightly and was rotating from side to side so that his fake tail wagged weakly back and forth.

'Good dog,' John said hoarsely, 'who's a good dog then? Is it you?'

The dog looked away from Pierre and moved slowly towards John, each huge paw the size of a dinner plate, padding silently closer.

John gave a squeak and tried to back up, but found himself pressed against a gorse bush. The dog dropped its head, sniffing the ground, and with great dignity and delicacy ate the cheese and onion pie that John had dropped to the floor.

'Good dog,' John whispered as the beast lifted its head again, 'who's a good boy then?'

The black dog gave a low growl.

'Oh hell,' muttered John, then realised that the dog was now looking past him. He half turned and noticed the sound of quiet voices carrying through the mist. He had been so focused on the black dog that he had not seen the glow of the approaching lantern.

'Customs men,' Pierre breathed, 'they must have heard us howling.'

'Stuck between a dog and a hard place,' muttered John. 'What do we do, Pierre?'

In one great bound the black dog was gone into the mist, leaving great gouges where his claws had dug into the soft earth.

'*Move! Now!*' Pierre hissed.

They grabbed everything up and fled as fast as their cumbersome load and costume allowed.

Yells of terror echoed through the night along with a roaring growl and the sounds of men crashing through the undergrowth.

'The black dog!'

'It's real!'

'Run for it, lads! Run for your lives!'

One particularly girlish scream echoed up the hill, but there were no sounds of men being savaged and no dying screams, only occasional panicked shouts echoed up to Pierre and John.

John, puffing and red-faced, his tail swinging wildly, eventually had to stop.

'They're gone Pierre. Slow down, please, I can't breathe.'

Pierre collapsed with a grunt, wheezing for breath. Reaching inside his costume, he plucked out his pipe and flung it as far from him as possible, pressing a hand to his chest and gritting his teeth as he fought to fill his burning lungs with breath.

John lay down on the cool ground, panting until he could speak again.

'Damn dog saved our hides, Pierre.'

'He did at that, John. Who's to say that he hadn't been planning to eat our hides just before that though?'

'He ate my pie, Pierre.'

'You missed out there, John. They were excellent pies. I baked them myself.'

'You do bake a fine pie, Pierre. I've always said so. You'll make some woman a fine husband one day.'

'He has excellent taste, that dog.'

'He's a good dog,' John said firmly, 'I knew it the moment he didn't kill us.'

Pierre nodded vigorously, 'A fine show of solidarity. We black dogs have to stick together. Who'd have thought it, John? The black dog of Bouley Bay! I never believed a word of the legend myself. If I hadn't seen it with my own eyes, eating my own pie, then I wouldn't believe it now.'

'Always believed in it, Pierre,' said John firmly, 'never doubted a word about it.'

The two men lay on the ground in silence, considering their encounter until eventually John propped himself up on one elbow.

'I tell you what, Pierre, all that running has left me right parched.'

'I'm spitting feathers myself, John,' Pierre said, producing the cup.

They drank a toast to the black dog of Bouley Bay, and it was the first of many.

THE VIOGE

As Alisa made her way up the steep hill of La Ruette à la Vioge, she mused upon its more common nickname of Crack Ankle Lane. The name was appropriate, although Alisa suspected more people probably broke bones falling on their way down the steep incline than plodding wearily up it as she was.

The narrow lane was as steep as a flight of steps, between a high field on one side and the slope of a wooded hill on the other. The pathway was really little more than a man-high grassy ditch, and with the arc of tree branches above her, Alisa found it like walking up a steep green tunnel.

As a young child, she had once tried to run down the hill. The steep slope had made it impossible for her to stop and her momentum had carried her, arms wheeling, until she tripped face first into the mud and slid to an ungainly stop. Winter ice and snow had left her sprawled on her backside more than once, but the far-off chill of winter was just a sweet memory to her now. She sweltered upwards in the heat of the summer sun, placing one foot determinedly in front of the other, trying to ignore the aching muscles of her legs.

Just a few more steps and she stopped at the same point where she had fallen in the mud as a child. Alisa clambered up the bank to the edge of the field and allowed herself a rest. From this high vantage point, she could look out over the sloping green fields to the huge curve of the bay of St Aubin. The sea was sparkling a heavenly blue under the clear sky above.

This marked what she always thought of as the halfway point of her daily slog back up the hill from her school in St Peter's Valley. She savoured the respite as she smiled at the glorious view and allowed herself to catch her breath. Her crop of fair hair was stuck to the back of her neck with perspiration. She wiped it with her hand, adjusting her necklace so that the tiny silver heart pendant, which had slipped around the chain, rested once again against her collarbone.

With a soft sigh, she slid back down the bank and regarded the narrow hill that led upwards towards her parents' house. Sitting and gazing out to sea wouldn't get her home any faster, and there were chores to be done. Alisa began her slow ascent once again.

A gentle breeze blew, cooling her neck. It carried the suggestion of a melody. It was almost familiar, like a memory of some long-loved tune that she could not place. She stopped and closed her eyes, straining to hear it, and for a moment the song hung in the air and then was lost as though carried away by a changing wind.

Turning, Alisa stood up on her tiptoes and looked out across the fields. She saw no one. There was only a scarecrow, hunched and filthy, its long arms splayed like broken wings. It stood in the field of growing wheat like a ragged statue in a rippling sea of green.

The source of the strange music was not apparent and Alisa wondered if she had imagined it. The rich coconut smell of gorse flowers filled her nostrils as the breeze stirred again, but there was no other sound than the whispering of grass and leaves. Even the birds had fallen silent.

With a weary shrug, Alisa walked on. Each step was an effort at the steepest part of the hill. She allowed herself to consider tumbling into bed when she reached her home for an afternoon doze. The thought was so appealing that she closed her blue eyes for a moment and heard the strange tune again. Her ears strained for it, her heart longed for it, and though her sudden weariness made the motion an effort, she lifted her head to look again for where it might be coming from. Her faltering steps had made almost no progress up the hill, she realised. The scarecrow was no further away than it had been. If anything, it appeared closer.

The melody was stronger now, and so very beautiful. Her steps slowed and feeling faint, she stumbled. Perhaps it was the heat. It had been a hot day in a stuffy classroom, after all. She hadn't had a glass of water since lunchtime. Dizzied, Alisa sank to her knees so that she would not fall. The haunting lullaby soothed her concerns. The smell of flowers was so strong. Perhaps if she rested briefly the sensation would pass and, while she rested, she could listen to the sweet tune upon the breeze. She lay still as a wave of exhaustion swept over her. A shadow moved to block the sun, but Alisa did not notice. Her eyes were already closed.

ᘓᗡᘉ

Alisa stirred from a deep sleep. She was resting on her back, comfortably numb and longing to drift back into total delirium, but there was something cold and uncomfortable at her throat. It was a tickling, chilling sensation, as though ice water was dripping onto her throat and was trickling down either side to pool at the nape of her neck. She struggled to lift one leaden arm and wiped her hand across her throat. Her fingers tingled as though they were brushing ice. It was her necklace she realised, her simple silver necklace, yet now it seemed alive like a thing of magic. She would have to remove it before she could fall asleep again.

Lifting her head, she fumbled at the clasp like a drunkard. Something shifted underneath her as though she were lying on a pile of branches. She was obviously not in her own bed, but was too tired to care overmuch.

Feeling rather as she had on the morning after she and Sally Le Maistre had finished her father's bottle of pear cider, Alisa tried to sit up, thinking only that she simply must remove her necklace. She forced her eyes open a crack and her vision was a blur. As her weight shifted so did her makeshift bed and she fell sharply a few inches, something jabbing painfully into her back. The jolt opened her eyes and Alisa realised that she was lying on a pile of bones. Some were ancient: yellow and brittle, turning to dust. Others were fresher, with gristle still clinging to them. Some were animal, but some were unmistakably human. Lines and scratches on the bones looked like claw marks. Or teeth marks.

With a gasp of horror, Alisa tried to get to her feet but stumbled as though drugged. Bones scattered as she tripped and landed in the filth, her face level with a grinning skull. The cloying smell of flowers that lingered on her clothes was corrupted with the sweet stench of rotted meat. Yet still the weariness tugged at her. The most ridiculous notion occurred to her, that if she could just lie back down and rest for a while, then she would be able to think more clearly about the danger she was in when she awoke. The grinning skull mocked her as her terror battled with the unnatural intoxication. Alisa understood that if she allowed herself to fall back to sleep, then she might never wake again. The necklace fell against her skin as she drew back from the skull and she grasped at the cool metal, this time in desperation. She tried to draw strength from it as she fought her way to a sitting position.

She was in a dark cave of some kind. Light filtered through a small gap ahead of her, enough to show her that the piles of bones covered the entire floor in shallow drifts. She retched to think that she had been laying in such gory filth.

'What is this place?' she whispered. She rubbed her necklace between her thumb and fingers, terrified that without it, she would once again submit to the delirium that had held her and become just another skeleton.

She lifted the heart pendant and slipped it into her mouth where it lay like a sliver of ice against her tongue. Her head cleared as though she had only now become fully awake. With her hands free, she braced herself and struggled to her feet, fighting against the dizziness that crashed over her like waves. She shuffled, first one foot and then the other, towards the source of the light, careful not to trip, wincing at each sound she made as bones rattled out a dry cacophony beneath her feet in the confines of the cave. She leant forward, low to the ground, her hands out in case she should fall. Her ears strained for any other sound than those that she was making herself. Someone or something had brought her here to this lair of ancient evil. If it returned, she needed to be ready. With this in mind, she reached for a length of bone, dry and yellowed with age and as thick as her wrist. A leg bone perhaps, whether it was that of a man or a beast she had no idea. She gripped and swung it, feeling the weight and heft of it. The bone seemed solid enough. If her captor returned, he would find himself confronting a girl ready to fight, rather than an unconscious victim.

The light shone through a gap low to the ground, curtained with thick ivy and carpeted in nettles. Alisa muttered quiet oaths when the nettles stung her legs and arms as she struggled through the clinging vegetation into the blinding light outside. The biting itch of the nettles dispelled her weariness even further.

'Where am I?' Alisa exclaimed as she staggered into the open, letting the heart pendant slip from her lips.

She had emerged under a canopy of trees, between two great tree roots that were almost invisible from the outside. Blinking to clear her vision, Alisa squinted around until she saw a break in the trees and moved towards it, out into the bright sunlight. Away down to her right was the blue sparkle of the sea. In front of her, a green field of young wheat. The slope of the land gave Alisa her bearings. She was only a stone's throw from where she last remembered walking, although the sun was markedly lower than it had been, indicating that she had slept for perhaps four hours in the cave of bones.

Ahead of her, across the shimmering field of waist-high wheat, would be the deep ditch of Crack Ankle Lane and the way home. Gripping her bone weapon to her chest, Alisa made her way as swiftly as she could across the field, wading into the green wheat as though she stepped into shark-infested waters. She kept the woods to her left, watching carefully for any movement beneath the trees, trying not to imagine monsters grabbing at her legs from beneath the green blanket of the farmer's crop.

The figure of a man caught her eye to the right. She inhaled sharply, meaning to cry out for help, then realised that it was just the scarecrow. The gaunt figure reminded her of the corpses in the cave. With a shudder, she hurried away from it as fast as she could, pushing through the whispering wheat and stumbling as she neared the deep ditch of Crack Ankle Lane. Brambles edged the field and she slowed, looking for a gap so that she could descend to the path below.

A soft note touched the breeze, and before she could stop herself, Alisa was straining to hear it. The melody hit her like a blow to the knees and she felt herself stagger in sudden exhaustion. Her bone weapon weighed down her arms and she let it fall, knowing there was no way she could fight with such a weight of weariness upon her.

She dropped to her hands and knees as the tune grew louder and the smell of gorse flowers filled her lungs, a rich and intoxicating scent, tinged unmistakably now with the stink of decay.

Gritting her teeth, Alisa struggled onwards. She crawled like a drunk, careless now of brambles beneath her hands. She welcomed the thorns that entered the soft flesh of her fingers in her battle to stay conscious.

She glanced back to see that the scarecrow was closer. It was closer again with a second glance, yet never in motion. Terrified to take her eyes from it, Alisa turned and struggled backwards on the heels of her palms, scrambling away from the thing, watching the black hollows of its eyes for some sign of life. The creature's mouth opened, the grey maw of a corpse, and again the beautiful song rang in her ears.

Alisa shouted a wordless yell, trying to drown out the creature's song with a scream of defiance as she fought her way backwards. Her hands reached into nothing, and with a gasp, Alisa fell backwards through the brambles and down the bank. Thorns lashed her face and caught at her clothes, wrenching her sideways before they snapped, so that she landed with a rolling jolt. She lay stunned for a moment, then struggled into a painful crawl. She began forcing one hand in front of the other up the narrow lane, her knees skinned and sore. Each contact with the ground fired pain through her body, keeping her awake. She glanced up and back and sobbed with terror to see the scarecrow standing on the ridge of the bank. Its empty eyes were fixed upon her, its claws curled in anticipation. She struggled onwards without taking her eyes from it and, as it opened its ragged mouth to sing once more, she reached for her necklace.

It was gone.

Alisa clawed at her own throat desperately. Even as she did so the sun caught on the silver heart where it hung, tangled in the brambles where she had fallen through. It spun slowly, glittering out of reach.

The song of the Vioge fell across her like a warm blanket.

As she laid her head on the stony ground, Alisa forgot why she was fighting so hard to keep her eyes open, and slipped gently away into darkness.

SACRED GROUND

He woke to the sound of knocking. There were two distinct rhythms of sound. One was an urgent staccato knuckle rapping and the other a polite, soft thumping. As Tom Grondin's head cleared enough for him to feel the pounding of his hangover join the cacophony, he began to make out voices.

'Mr Grondin?'

'Boss, are you there? Are you awake?'

Tom glanced at his clock and gave a grunt of displeasure. His celebratory tipple of the night before had turned into a few celebratory glasses, and after that things were a little hard to remember. He eyed the empty bottle of claret on the table with a grimace.

'I'm coming damn it!' he croaked as the knocking continued.

He and his men had broken ground on the site for the new church in the parish of St Brelade the day before. The work had gone well and the weather had been fine. He had left instructions for the men to continue without him so that he could take a little extra rest this morning. He found he often needed it these days.

'What?' he demanded, throwing the door open against the wall with a bang and squinting painfully into the sunlight.

Clement Le Vech, the laconic French architect, and James awaited him. James was young and new to his team. He looked scruffy next to the elegant Frenchman.

'What is it?' Tom asked in a less gruff tone as he tried to smooth the grey furze of his hair. 'What's happened?'

'Maybe we should ask you the same?' Clement ventured, raising an eyebrow.

The two men looked at him curiously for a few moments and then exchanged glances.

'He doesn't know,' James said.

'What don't I know?' Tom sighed, feeling his patience begin to wear thin.

'Perhaps you should get dressed, Mr Grondin,' Clement said calmly, 'there is something that you need to see.'

Tom Grondin returned inside, muttering under his breath. He splashed water on his face, stared into the reflection of his bloodshot blue eyes, then threw yesterday's clothes and boots on. He soon joined them in the cart, but neither Clement nor James would offer any information as to why they felt he needed to be taken back to the site.

'It's strange, boss,' James said, his brown eyes serious, 'you need to see for yourself really.'

Clement Le Vech kept his eyes on the horse as he drove.

Tom sat in simmering annoyance as the cart bounced and rumbled along the track. He tried to imagine what manner of idiocy his workers could possibly have contrived, in the few hours since dawn broke, that could necessitate the presence of the overseer. The sunlight was so bright that he found the short journey bearable only by bowing his head and resting his face in the palms of his hands. A feeling of nausea began to grow.

'We're here,' James said as the cart rumbled to a halt.

'We're where?' Tom yawned and looked around at his twenty men, standing or sitting quietly, looking at him expectantly.

'Where's the site?' he demanded.

Clement stared at him and James shrugged as he said, 'That's the thing, boss, we don't know.'

Tom stepped slowly out of the cart and walked to the centre of the grassy clearing. Here they had paced out the measurements the day before. They had stripped the turf, dug trenches and begun to lay foundation stones. Here, yesterday, there had been a building site with piles of stone ready to build the beautiful new church that Clement Le Vech had designed. Now there was only the peaceful glade, exactly as it had been months ago when it had been selected as the site for the church.

'Where is everything?' he demanded of his men.

A wave of shrugs and raised palms greeted his enquiry.

'Is this supposed to be a joke?' he asked suspiciously. 'I am not in the mood for jokes.'

He continued to glare at his men, but as none of them broke down and confessed to anything, there was little more that he could do. Tom sighed in exasperation.

'How could anyone move all the damn stones and equipment during the night anyway? Have you looked around? It can't be far, it must–'

'Ha! I knew it,' Effy Tostevin stood on the edge of the clearing with her arms folded, smiling broadly and nodding in satisfaction.

'You knew what?' Tom asked in irritation at being interrupted.

'I knew they wouldn't let you build here.'

Effy continued to nod sagely, looking around to make sure she had everyone's full attention.

'I knew it. I even said so to Mary, I said, "Mary, you mark my words, they'll *never* let them build it there," and she said, "Well, now why's that then, Effy?" and I said, "Well, Mary–"'

Tom cut her off by shouting, '*Who* wouldn't let us build here? Was this La Ferac's work? I swear I'll have the constable down on him so fast …'

'Well,' Effy said, regarding him with lofty disdain, 'I'm sure I don't know who you're talking about. It's like I said to Mary, I said, "Mary, that's sacred fairy ground right there where they've chosen to build that church, and you mark my words, those fairies won't have it, they *will not have it*, they'll never let them build there, you mark my words," that's what I said, you can ask her yourself.'

She nodded firmly and then inhaled sharply as she caught sight of James.

'What would your old grandma have said if she knew you were disrespecting the fairies like this, James Filleul?' she demanded. 'She'll spin in her grave!'

'She won't. I never did,' James protested weakly, 'I didn't. What fairies?'

Effy was still shaking her head in dismay as a shout rang out from the trees.

'Found it!' John Le Vesconte trotted into the clearing with a sheen of sweat across his brow, 'I've found it all down by the fishermen's chapel on the far side of the bay.'

Tom looked at him in disbelief, 'But that's … that's nearly a mile away! How in the name of God did anybody manage to move that amount of stone and equipment in a single night?'

John shrugged, 'No idea boss, but they did. What now?'

'Well,' Tom heaved a heavy sigh, 'I suppose we go and bloody get it all again, don't we?'

The men grumbled and shuffled their feet as they began to move.

'If you want my advice,' Effy Tostevin said, folding her arms, 'you'll leave it where it all is. They won't let you build here, it's like I said to Mary.'

It took until dusk to bring the necessary equipment and stone back to the site. Effy had left the site with much tutting and shaking of her head at around lunchtime and Tom had never been gladder to see the back of anyone.

'We'll have to get the rest of it tomorrow,' he said. His head was pounding and he needed a drink, 'I can't have men stumbling about in the dark all along the coast. Half the boys can start digging the foundations in the morning, and the rest can go for what's left at the chapel. At least none of the tools were stolen or damaged, but I swear when I get my hands on whoever did this …'

'What about tonight?' James asked.

'What *about* tonight?' Tom said before he realised what the boy was asking and was startled. 'You think they'd pull the same prank two nights on the trot? Surely not.'

James shrugged and looked down at his dusty, cut hands, 'Well I certainly wouldn't have the energy for it. I'm sure it will be fine. Good night, boss. I'll see you in the morning.'

'Yes, good night, James.'

Tom looked over at the piles of stone that they had carried back up from along the bay. As he made his way home the notion that a repeat performance of the prank was a possibility hastened his steps. He made himself a quick dinner, drank a couple of glasses of wine, and gradually a determined expression settled on his face.

'Make a damn fool of me, will you?' he muttered.

Taking the half-empty bottle, he left the house and made his way back to the site. All the way there he rehearsed in his mind the speech he would make when he found La Ferac's men attempting to move his stones once more. He would cry out against the injustice of denying an honest man an honest wage, and La Ferac would plead with him not to call the constable. The thought brought a smile to Tom's face and he was almost disappointed when he arrived back at the site to find everything exactly as he had left it.

'Still,' he muttered, 'best to be on the safe side,' and settling down against a tree at the edge of the clearing, he slowly finished his bottle of wine and fell asleep.

'Boss?'

Tom awoke with a start and winced at the pain in his back.

'Did you see who it was then?' James asked hopefully.

'Did I see who what …' Tom trailed off as he looked around.

The site was clear. Every last stone and tool was missing from where it had been the night before and a few of his men were standing around smoking.

Clement toed the empty wine bottle lying next to Tom's leg and raised his eyebrows pointedly.

'We'll take that as a *no* then,' he said quietly.

James smiled and shrugged, 'What do we do now then, boss?'

A delighted gasp from behind him made Tom turn uncomfortably, and then groan at the sight of Effy Tostevin.

'Well,' she said with relish, 'I knew you wouldn't pay me any mind. It's just like I said to myself last night, I said to myself, "Effigina, they'll not pay you the least bit of mind. You wait and see, it'll be the same thing all over again tomorrow and they'll just all be stood around like great lumps of men, thinking they know better than a woman, but they don't,"' she shook her head and added by way of clarification, 'You don't.'

'Men,' Tom called, ignoring her, 'start fetching the stones and tools back up, same as yesterday. If La Ferac's men can move them twice, then so can we. I'll be back later.'

As he left he could hear Effy Tostevin relating what she had said to Mary on the subject of the building site, as well as the ill-concealed grumbling of his men. He was too tired and angry to care. Reaching his house he tumbled into bed.

Just before dusk he returned to the site feeling refreshed but in need of a drink. Many of his men had already left and he didn't really blame them. The pile of recovered stone was smaller than it had been the day before and piled more carelessly.

'Time for home, gentlemen,' Tom called, noting with relief that Effy was nowhere to be seen.

James, visibly exhausted, gave him a questioning look.

'I'll keep watch tonight,' Tom said, then added, 'properly this time. I wasn't really expecting them last night, but I'll be ready for them this time.'

'Do you want me to stay, boss?'

'No, son, you need your rest. Get off home now. I'll see you in the morning.'

As his men left the site Tom made a great show of looking around and then, as though he was pleased with what he saw, he made as though to leave. Walking briefly in the direction of his home in case anybody was watching him from the trees, he soon ducked back quietly and peered around. Climbing carefully into the low branches of an elm tree, Tom was confident that he was well concealed yet he had an excellent view of the site. He was very uncomfortable so there would be very little chance of him falling asleep. Using anger to fuel his energy he settled back against the tree trunk to wait.

The hours slipped past interminably. As the distant sound of St Peter's church bells drifted almost inaudibly across the night, Tom became more and more certain that his tormentors would not

come back. Eleven o'clock struck and Tom shifted to try and ease
the pain of his back. Surely there would not even be time for anyone
to move the tools and stones before his men returned in the morning.
Yet a fear of greater humiliation, should he miss the culprits again,
made him grit his teeth and remain in the tree. He was desperate
for a drink. How long had it been since he'd gone an evening without at least one bottle of wine after his meal? A few years at least.
He closed his eyes and rested as best he could, letting his mind
wander. Dwelling on the church that he would build, he let it take
shape in his mind; laying the foundations, raising the walls, seeing
it as it would be upon completion. He toyed with the complexi-
ties he would face, areas which would be problematic and would
require more skilled hands than the younger men had. He smiled
gently. It would be a fine structure. People would admire it. Clement
Le Vech was an artist, but Tom Grondin was the man who would

make that artist's pretty pictures solid and immortal. The church would stand for thousands of years if it was built right, and Tom intended to see that it was built right, no matter what discomfort he had to go through. No matter what nonsense he had to put up with.

In the distance, the church bells rang out the midnight hour.

And then they came.

He saw the woman first. The White Lady shone as though moonlight emanated from her pale skin and clothing. She was tall and slender. Her hair fell almost to her knees and was the soft gold of sunlight while her eyes were the rich brown of fertile earth.

As she walked the host followed after her. They were full of grace, their movements silent in the still air. Men and women of delicate sylvan beauty, and other, smaller creatures, flitting here and there. Strange beasts moved with them, and a huge black dog as big as a bear stepped from the shadows to stand at the White Lady's side protectively.

On the other side of the clearing, shadows detached from the trees. They were led by a handsome man in dark clothing with hair like midnight and a cruel mouth. A few of these shadows walked with the same elegance as their master, but these creatures were more stealthy than graceful. Some seemed to shift before Tom's vision. Others were twisted and misshapen in a way that turned his stomach to ice water. Stunted things the size of children crept across the ground or danced madly. Crooked things and monsters of horrifying variety made him glad that he could not see them any better under the shadows of the trees.

Tom's breath caught in his throat as the two groups faced each other across the glade, light and dark, like figures upon a chessboard.

'Lord Regent,' The woman greeted her dark counterpart.

Her voice was like a spring breeze. It made Tom smile through his fears. To have heard the voice of the White Lady. Was there another mortal man alive who could make such a claim?

'So here we are again then,' the tall man said to the White Lady. His voice was rich as syrup but chilled Tom to the bone.

'Yes, Lord Regent. What's the matter? Do you grow weary of moving stones?'

'I do actually,' replied the Regent, 'especially when there are easier ways to dissuade humans from their folly. A few less of them wouldn't harm this island in the slightest. This place has been sacred since before men here, since before it was an island at all. How many times are we going to have to do this before those imbeciles leave this place alone?'

'As many times as it takes,' the White Lady said, 'and if the Unseelie Court would rather not participate, then my people–'

'This place is as sacred to us as it is to you,' the Regent interrupted, 'I am simply saying that some kind of punishment should be meted out for this violation of–'

'I am aware of your arguments, Regent,' her voice suddenly rang with power and Tom ducked down as though a blow had been aimed at him.

The White Lady stepped forward and Tom was surprised that the Regent didn't back away as she continued, 'There would be no greater sacrilege to this place than to spill blood upon its soil. I will not countenance it. Now, shall we begin?'

The Regent made a dismissive gesture and his dark host began to bound towards the stones that Tom's men had spent their whole day returning from the shore by the fishermen's chapel.

The White Lady raised one imperious finger and the elegant members of her company joined the dark fae in their toil.

Tom thought that the White Lady and the Regent might simply glare at each other throughout the entire procedure, but at length the White Lady smoothed her skirts.

'I see that the Prince and the Princess have wearied of this?' she remarked softly.

The Regent grinned, looking suddenly younger and less threatening.

'Nothing upon the land is sacred to the ocean children of Ahès Dahut, my Lady. Once the prospect of killing the humans was removed as a possibility, they returned to their castle with their wolves.'

'They may challenge you for the Unseelie Throne one day, Lord Regent,' the White Lady warned.

The Regent's smile grew almost unnaturally wide.

'They are welcome to try,' he said adjusting his cuffs with his long white fingers, 'I believe I am capable of dealing with the twins. However I trust that, should it come to it, I would have your support, my Lady?'

The White Lady's eyebrows lifted slightly.

'You know it would not be appropriate for me to interfere in the concerns of the Unseelie Court, Lord Regent.'

'Of course not, Your Highness.'

Tom thought perhaps the White Lady gave the Regent a hint of a smile, but then she turned away as though she wished to watch the diminishing mountain of stone.

A strange form from the dark side of the court had made its way to the base of the pile of rocks. A woman, Tom thought, yet her form seemed to shift before his eyes. He could have sworn that she was a young and lovely girl with glossy chestnut hair, but then the moonlight illuminated a dirty twisted creature who seemed more formed from tree roots than flesh. As Tom watched she reached her arms between the stones and seemed to flow, like bindweed growing before his eyes. She diminished from the form of a woman and extended in a tangle of vines, twisting and wrapping herself among the rocks until she was all but invisible within the stones. The rest of the court stood back expectantly.

For a moment all was still, and then the pile of rocks shifted and began to move. Stones tumbled from the pile and rolled away like unwanted material under a sculptor's chisel. The humanoid form of a stone golem, taller than any man, broke from the rubble and marched with the heavy crunch and grind of rock upon rock across the clearing.

Tom realised that his mouth was hanging open as the elemental creature passed before his hiding place, shaking the branches of his tree as it moved with each thunderous step.

'God in Heaven,' he whispered.

The Regent whipped his head around and turned, seeming to stare straight at him. Tom froze, his blood running cold in his veins as the Regent's dark, predatory eyes looked straight through him.

He was certain he had been seen. Then the Regent frowned as though confused and looked away, watching as the last of the stones were gathered up by the dark and light fae and whisked off with ease towards the fishermen's chapel.

'And we're done,' said the Regent as he and the White Lady were left alone, 'Shall we go, my Lady?'

'You go on, Lord Regent,' she said, 'I wish to remain for a few moments alone in this place.'

The Regent bowed deeply, almost mockingly, and with a smile he said, 'No doubt I shall see you at the same time tomorrow night?'

'No, I believe this will be the last night,' the White Lady said, 'fare thee well, Regent.'

He raised a dark brow, but when she did not expand upon her suspicion he shrugged.

'Good night then, my Lady. You know where to find me. Should you want me. A delight to see you, as always.'

The White Lady looked slightly perplexed.

'Thank you, Regent,' she said uncertainly.

With his unnaturally white smile gleaming in the moonlight, the Regent turned and departed. As he left the shadows receded.

Tom drew air into his lungs as though a weight had been lifted from his chest.

The White Lady closed her eyes and lifted her palms. Subtle changes occurred around her as she whispered words too soft for Tom to hear. The grass rippled as though a strong breeze stirred. The bruised earth lifted and flattened as though the huge golem had never passed and the blades of grass had never been crushed. The wave of energy expanded outwards and passed through Tom who suddenly felt awake and alive in a way that he had not since his youth. The pain in his back disappeared and his limbs were no longer stiff. The thirst for wine was gone, as though it had never been.

'You can come out now,' the White Lady said gently.

Tom stayed very still, afraid to breathe.

'The gentleman in the tree,' the White Lady clarified patiently. 'There's no point closing your eyes. Just because you can't see me, doesn't mean that I can't see you.'

Tom swallowed and carefully lowered himself from the branches to the ground. With a few swift breaths, he tried to find his courage, then stepped out into her light.

'My Lady,' he said awkwardly as he lowered himself to one knee.

'There is no need for that, human. You owe me no fealty.'

Tom looked up at her uncertainly. It seemed deeply disrespectful to stand as an equal to the Queen of the Fairies.

'I'd rather stay down here if it's alright with you, Your Majesty,' he said carefully.

She laughed gently, the loveliest sound that Tom had ever heard, and he smiled at her.

'Do stand up, human. Tell me your name please.'

'Thomas, my Lady,' Tom said, getting awkwardly to his feet. 'I am the overseer of the ...' Tom waved his hand vaguely around the clearing. 'I am so terribly sorry for the inconvenience we've put you to. Had I known, I would never have tried to build here. I didn't believe ...'

He trailed off as the White Lady quirked a brow in amusement.

'You didn't believe we exist?'

'Yes, my Lady,' Tom admitted, shuffling his feet awkwardly.

'I imagine you feel somewhat differently now.'

'Yes, my Lady.'

'You may not build your temple here, Thomas. Will I need to return tomorrow night?'

'No, Your Majesty! I'll see that you aren't troubled any further. How long did you know that I was here?'

'I feel the life of every creature around me from the birds in the sky to the insects in the grass. A man hiding in a tree wasn't going to escape my notice, Thomas.'

'But the others didn't know?'

'I shielded you from their sight. I rather thought it might complicate the evening if the Unseelie Court were aware of you.'

'Yes,' said Tom, a shiver running down his spine, 'yes, I think you're right. Thank you for that, my Lady.'

'You are most welcome.'

'Why is this place sacred to you, Your Majesty? There is nothing here, after all.'

The White Lady smiled.

'There is nothing that you can see. But there is something deep beneath the earth that once was marked with stones; something which rests. Believe me when I say, it would be in the best interests of your race to leave it undisturbed. Forever.'

'Yes, my Lady.'

'I am glad that we have reached an accord, Thomas. I shall take my leave of you now.'

'Yes, my Lady,' Tom said sadly, 'I suppose I won't see you again?'

The White Lady smiled kindly.

'I suppose not, Thomas,' she hesitated, and then added, 'There is a young tree beside the new site at the coast. If left undisturbed she will grow into a creature of great power and beauty in the grounds of the church. Will you see that she is not harmed, Thomas?'

'I will see to it, my Lady.'

'Then perhaps I will come and look upon this temple when it is complete.'

Thomas bowed low to the ground, and then watched the light of the White Lady recede as she walked slowly into the trees and was lost to view.

He made his way down to the old fishermen's chapel at the end of the bay and put his hands on his hips. Narrowing his eyes, he considered the site. The land was flat and even. The ground was good. He soon spied the tree that the White Lady had spoken of: a young sapling standing alone in the area that would be the graveyard. Ordinarily he would have pulled it up without a moment's thought, but now he walked over to it and gently touched its leaves.

He was still sitting beside it with a smile on his face, looking out over the beauty of St Brelade's Bay, when James and Clement Le Vech arrived at dawn in the cart.

'This is a good site,' he said to them as they pulled up, the horse snorting and rolling its eyes as though it smelled something troubling.

'This? Beside the sea?' Clement pulled a face, 'It's a much longer walk from the village.'

'It will do the people good to take a stroll,' Tom stood up and brushed off his trousers. 'Besides, it turns out we don't really have a choice in the matter.'

'Did you see who did it?' James asked, 'Was it La Ferac's men?'

'No, it wasn't La Ferac's men.'

'Was it …' James shook his head then and grinned. 'Well it wasn't fairies, so who was it?'

'This sapling needs to stay,' Tom said firmly. 'James, see to it that all the men know that this tree must be protected during the building. It's very important.'

'It's so close,' Clement protested, 'Surely–'

'It must be protected,' Tom reiterated firmly. 'She will grow to be beautiful. She will be beside the church forever and they will complement each other, something made by man and something made by nature, existing in harmony.'

'Have you been drinking again?' Clement raised an eyebrow.

'No,' Tom said flashing him a look. 'No, I shan't be drinking any more. Oh dear God,' he added as he caught sight of Effy Tostevin approaching along the beach.

'Didn't I tell you?' she called from the distance, 'Didn't I say?'

'Yes and you were quite right, Effy,' he called back, 'we're going to build it here instead now.'

'Fairies?' she shouted.

With a sigh and a glance at James and Clement Le Vech, Tom shrugged and nodded.

'Yes, Effy!' he shouted back, 'Fairies!'

Then lower, so that only James could hear, he added, 'If that woman stands around for more than five minutes, put a shovel in her hand and get her digging until she's out of breath, or so help me I will bury her in the foundations.'

THE FIVE SPANISH SHIPS

In the ancient days, before the rising of the ocean, the island of Jersey was larger and bordered to the west by rich forest in the parish of St Ouen. The trees clustered along the coast and stirred in the wild winds that blew in from the bay of Mont St Michel.

One night it so happened that a treacherous storm arose as five Spanish ships were attempting to traverse the English Channel. The Spanish barques carried fine wines and spices, rich fabrics and all the wealth of their passengers.

The largest of the ships, *The Raven*, rode low in the water so laden was it with the iron-bound chests of its owner. The Captain of this ship was grateful for its weight for the first time, since the cargo that had slowed their entire coterie now protected them slightly from the capricious fury of the storm.

Wild winds tossed the other boats like toys upon the powerful waves that threatened to swamp or capsize them. They floundered hopelessly. It was all the helmsmen could do to prevent the boats from crashing into one another. Their lanterns blazed through the driving rain so that each could see the others and try to adjust course before they were forced too close.

The mast of one ship crashed to the deck, snapped clean off by the force of the wind. Lanterns smashed, spraying oil across the deck where fire blazed and roared into the rigging before a wave doused the flames. Flapping sails and ropes were washed overboard by the receding water. Sailors cried out as the tangle wrapped around them and they were hauled into the sea as though the ocean itself were casting a net for them.

The Captain of *The Raven* clung to the wheel, his face grim. He knew that they had been blown off course and out of sight of the French coast, yet there was nothing that he and his compatriots could do except hope to ride out the storm. If there was safe harbour to be found, it was hidden by the moonless night.

When he saw lights and torches spring up in the distance he almost sobbed aloud for joy to see them begin to illuminate the line of a shore that he had not even known was there. Perhaps after all they would find a port in this storm.

The dancing torchlights were joined by the great blaze of a bonfire on the shoreline. In front of its flickering flames, he could just make out the figures of men seeming to dance strangely in the moving light as they beckoned to the ships. Their words were lost on the wind and drowned out by the crashing of the waves, but the message was clear: the sailors should guide the ships in towards them to find safety from the storm.

'Where are we? What is this place?' The first mate cried as he lurched across the heaving deck and clung to the ship's wheel beside the Captain.

'This cannot be England, surely?'

'No,' the Captain shook his head, 'we are still too far to the south. There were islands upon the map. Perhaps this is one of those? Jersey was the most southerly and the largest of them.'

'Are we saved then? Will they guide us to shore?'

'We are saved, Alvaro. See there, where the lights are swaying up high, above the shoreline? They must have lit lanterns in the other ships in the harbour to show us the way!'

As he turned from the helm he saw that the other ships in their fleet of five had also seen the lights and were busy raising their sails. Even the struggling barque that had lost a mast was trying to raise canvas.

'How are our passengers?'

'The little girl is afraid, but her father comforts her. He told her land is close by.'

'How did he know?'

The first mate met the Captain's surprised gaze and shrugged. 'Who knows with that one?'

The Captain smiled, 'You fear him, don't you, Alvaro?'

Alvaro gave a shaky laugh, 'You don't?'

'Not anymore,' the Captain said firmly.

He remembered quite clearly how he had initially shared his first mate's trepidation of their passenger, Senor Pietra. The man was an imposing sight: head and shoulders taller than most, with the rich dark skin and fine bones of an Egyptian. The merchant's black eyes had seemed to look through the Captain upon their first meeting, and the old sailor had found himself offering a far more generous deal for passage to the North than he had ever intended. There was a power about Pietra, despite his polite manner and elegant bearing, something that the Captain had not encountered before. It had seemed almost sinister at first.

Senor Pietra's daughter was another matter entirely however. The child was in her thirteenth year, strikingly lovely with long curls the colour of ebony and a wide grin that rarely left her face. On their first day from shore, the child had appeared at the Captain's elbow and laid one finger tentatively upon the wheel.

'Hello, Senor Captain. Please teach me how to steer the ship,' she had requested without a hint of shyness.

'And why would you wish to know how to steer a ship, young Neroli?' the Captain had laughed, tousling her dark curls.

'My father says that all knowledge is of value,' Neroli replied promptly. 'Besides, I might wish to be a sailor myself one day.'

The Captain was about to point out to the girl how unlikely a scenario this would be, but instead he had chosen to step aside and show the child where to place her hands on the wheel.

'You are quite right, young miss,' he said with a little bow, 'I am sure you will make a very fine sailor indeed. A captain before you are twenty years old I imagine.'

He had accidently caught Senor Pietra's eye then, and his imposing passenger had given him a smile and a nod of thanks.

'My own daughter must never find out about this however,' the Captain had added.

Pietra had laughed, and in that moment they had become friends.

Staggering against the force of the wind the first mate left the Captain's side to bark orders at the men. The howl of the storm stole his words, but the sailors knew their ship well and moved almost instinctively to set the sails.

Peering through the driving rain the Captain saw similar activity on the other ships and he allowed himself to hope that they would soon all be safe. The three undamaged ships were already in motion and moving closer to shore. His own weighted barque would be slower and more unwieldy, so he would follow them in so as not to slow their course.

'What is happening?'

The Captain jumped as his tall merchant passenger appeared at his side.

'Senor Pietra! You would be safer below deck with your daughter, sir.'

The passenger's dark eyes stared through the night, unblinking against the harsh wind.

'She is scared, Captain. What can I tell her?'

The Captain pointed towards the shore.

'See there, Senor Pietra? Where the lights are lit above the bonfire? I believe the people of this island are showing us the lights in their own ships' rigging, trying to guide us into their harbour that we may find our way to safety until the storm passes.'

Pietra nodded and his black eyes met the Captain's.

'I shall bring Neroli up that she may see them. She is not used to the ocean or to confined spaces. She is a child of earth and stone and desert. The lights will calm her when she sees how close she is to having her feet upon solid ground once again. Are we safe then? Can you guide us into the harbour despite this storm?'

'I believe so, sir. Though we will be the last in to port.'

'That is well,' Pietra nodded, 'there are more men upon the other ships, are there not?'

'Yes, Senor Pietra, and we are larger and slower for having a heavier cargo.'

Pietra's dark gaze did not waver as he said to the Captain, 'My daughter is all that matters to me, Captain. She is more valuable than all the treasures of the earth. If you need to lighten our load; have your men dump the gold over the side.'

The Captain gaped and then recovered himself. He had suspected that their cargo had been too heavy to be anything else, but to hear it confirmed shocked him. A king's ransom in his humble hold.

'I am certain that will not be necessary, Senor,' he managed to say, 'I can guide us in regardless of the extra weight. If anything our weight gives us more stability. I will do everything within my power to bring little Neroli safe to shore. You have my word.'

Pietra gripped the Captain's shoulder with his strong fingers and nodded. Then he turned and forged back through the waves washing across the deck to the cabin he shared with his child.

Turning from his passenger, the Captain noticed that the damaged barque was struggling. He watched, his expression grim, as the ship with the broken mast was broadsided by a great wave and slowly turned turtle. She began to sink beneath the onslaught of the churning waters, and as her lights extinguished the sight of her sailors struggling to swim was lost to the darkness. Only four ships remained, but they were gathering momentum as the waves drove them hard for shore.

The first of the ships had almost reached the dancing lights when the sound of a cracking impact was heard above the wind. For a moment the Captain thought it was thunder, and then he saw the lead ship buckle and tilt.

'What happened?' Pietra demanded, back at his side, this time with his daughter in his arms.

Neroli's eyes were wild with fear and she clung to her father.

'The *Red Sky* struck rock,' the Captain said in horror, pointing to the lead ship as it listed to its side. 'But how can that be?'

The *Red Sky* tilted, its keel lifting into the air as the rolling waves forced her high onto the invisible rocks beneath the water's surface, and then the movement of the ocean tore the boat away again, gutting her stem to stern.

The cries of her sailors rang through the night as the relentless tide drove another ship onto a hidden reef, crushing the bow with the force of impact. Sailors were flung overboard and from the rigging.

'God help us, it's a trap,' the Captain whispered. Then he roared, 'Hard about men! All hands! We're being led onto the rocks!'

As his men leapt to obey his commands, he watched helplessly as a third ship to shore fought to slow its speed, their own Captain screaming orders as he too realised that there was no safe harbour to be found. His ship jerked and tilted sideways as the sharp points of a reef beneath tore into the keel. It was lodged, the battering waves began to rock the barque as they pounded her hull, scraping the boat relentlessly against stone, tearing out the underside of her as though stone teeth were grinding her timbers. The ship behind them, unable to slow its momentum or turn, ploughed into them, crushing the boat and its men and piercing its own hull on the reef.

They began to sink almost immediately, sailors and passengers threw themselves into the merciless sea to avoid being dragged down with their vessel and were cruelly thrown against rocks and sub-merged by mountainous waves.

'Wreckers!' the Captain spat as he stared again at the dancing lights. He could now make out lanterns raised on poles to mimic lights in the rigging of boats in a harbour.

'Why would they do this?' Senor Pietra asked in horror.

'They are drawing us onto the rocks to destroy the ships so that they can salvage our cargo when we are destroyed.'

A thump and a scraping sound beneath them turned the Captain's blood to ice as hidden rocks beneath the waves caressed the side of the ship. It was as though some great beast were testing its claws against their hull.

'Do something, father!' Neroli cried out, her eyes wild as a trapped animal.

'I have no power over the water or the air, my child,' Pietra said, holding her tighter, 'I cannot control the waves or the wind.'

The merchant looked desperately to the Captain, who tried not to let the terror show on his own features. He kept his hands steady on the wheel as his men trimmed sails and hauled ropes with a flawless efficiency which was still no match for the driving wind and the powerful push of the tide. They dropped off the peak of one great wave and slammed against rock, not hard enough to crack the hull, but with enough force to throw one of the sailors from the rigging.

The Captain gritted his teeth as he turned the wheel away from that reef, holding them steady, uncertain whether he would be guiding them directly into another hidden trap.

Neroli sobbed as a gentle impact nudged them to starboard. The Captain swallowed, his mouth dry with fear, and kept his hands light on the wheel as the first mate roared orders. The ship and crew were in perfect symbiosis, sailing blind as they were forced ever closer to shore, slow, but not slow enough to protect them if the waves forced them onto the rocks.

'There are rocks to the left,' Pietra said softly.

The Captain steered away from a patch of water that looked no more dangerous than any other did to him.

'Did you see them break the surface?' he asked.

'I feel them beneath the water,' Pietra said.

The merchant had his eyes closed. His face creased with concentration.

'There are rocks everywhere. I should have sensed this, but the storm ... we must turn around! There is no safe path to shore, and even if there were these men will likely kill us when we reach it.'

'The tide will not let us turn back,' the Captain admitted to him, and as he met the merchant's eyes again, he could not hide his despair.

They could make out the forms of the wreckers now; the men of the island seemed almost to walk on water as they leapt from rock to rock near the shore, coming closer, eager to see this last ship torn apart on the reefs.

A huge wave smashed across the deck and Neroli cried out.

The closer they were driven towards the visible rocks and the nearer they came to the roaring white of the breakers, the more the rise and fall of the waves caused the boat to submit to the pitch and yaw of the rolling ocean. The Captain's attempts to steer became more futile, it was all that he could do to keep the waves behind them so that they did not smash against the side of the boat and tip them over. Then the tide pulled back and a wave lifted them high upon its peak as it began to break into white water. They were caught in the surf and with a huge surge of speed the breaking wave drove them like a carriage harnessed with white horses. Out of control they roared forward and then slammed hard with a tremendous force of impact against the rocks. The Captain gasped as he felt his ribs crack against the wheel. His men were tossed to the deck like rag dolls, yet somehow the merchant kept his feet as though he were rooted to the ship.

The front of the weighted barque was pushed high out of the water at an impossible angle. For a moment the Captain thought the force of the waves would carry *The Raven* all the way over, then they wedged between the points of two rocks and slowly the ship began to break apart, timbers cracking under the pressure of its own weight.

The stern began to tear away behind them. The merchant struggled forwards towards the figurehead and, holding his daughter against his chest with one strong arm, he reached down as far as he could over the side of the ship and brushed his fingers against the rocks on which they were wrecked.

A strange shudder ran through the timbers of the ship and, even as she continued to tear into two, her stern held fast between the rocks. Even as the masts came down around them, the pounding waves could not shift the front of the ship from where she was wedged.

The wreckers were creeping across the rocks that were high enough to protect them from the raging sea. Like spiders across a web, they moved in, cautious of their unknown prey.

With a mighty crack the back of the barque tore away from the front entirely, spilling cargo into the hungry mouth of the ocean, broken chests cascading gold as they slipped into the white water.

The Captain had the oddest idea that the merchant's fingertips were somehow anchoring them to the rocks as Pietra's voice rang across the night.

'People of this island, I beg of you: take my daughter. Save her! She is more precious to me and to the world than any fortune that you could steal from these ships.'

The wreckers did not respond, grinning and stirring like hungry dogs as they inched closer.

'Men of this island,' the merchant called again, and the Captain marvelled that his voice overrode the storm and the roaring waves, 'if you save my daughter I will freely give to you all that I have and more; a fortune beyond measure, and power beyond imagining. She is the last of our kind, the very last of the Land Singers. Make this deal with me, I beg.'

'We'll have everything that is yours anyway, fool, once your ship goes down,' one of the men shouted back. His compatriots cackled at this, but then the cracking of the timbers drowned out their laughter and shouts as the boat began to slip backward into the waves.

The great voice of Pietra boomed over all as he shouted to the wreckers one last time.

'I have begged of you and I have bargained with you. Now I curse you: Save my daughter or I shall tear your lives to ruins! One year from this day, I shall show you my vengeance. Show mercy now for my child and for yourselves. Take my daughter, or lose *everything*.'

'Just take her!' the Captain heard the words burst from his own lips as the timbers beneath his feet began to separate. 'What kind of monsters are you? Just save the child!'

But the wreckers did not respond and his voice was lost on the wind.

The last of the Spanish ships, *The Raven,* tore apart beneath them. As she slid from the jagged reef the merchant slammed his fist down against the rock with a wordless roar of hatred and turned from the wreckers. He covered Neroli's eyes and held her close as the raging sea swallowed the ship whole and threw them against the rocks to their doom.

༄

The tide receded, leaving a fortune in gold visible the next morning. There were raw nuggets taken straight from the earth of a far away land. The chunks of precious metal were surrounded by unusual pebbles, which the wreckers ignored as they scavenged the beach at low tide, not recognising gem stones in their raw and uncut form, nor able to tell them apart from the normal stones of the beach. They stepped without care over the bodies of drowned sailors, only stopping occasionally to check a man's pockets or tear a chain from a corpse's throat.

The wreckers laughed and celebrated, and fought and stole from one another. Then they traded, and drank and allowed their farms and livelihoods to fall to ruin, utterly indolent in their immeasurable wealth. They built their homes in sight of the sea on the rich and fertile land of St Ouen, and lived like kings without conscience, revelling in the wealth and fortune which they had bought at the expense of the lives which had been lost on the five Spanish ships.

As the months passed, those who had heard the merchant's curse soon forgot it. After all, what vengeance could a man whose corpse had long since washed ashore wreak upon the living?

The day came when they celebrated the anniversary of their good fortune, at the home of one Pierre Sauvage, the architect of their plan and the leader of their group before they had each gained so much.

A few nervous laughs and derisive comments were all that the memory of the merchant's curse occasioned, and expensive alcohol flowed freely. Their conversation was loud and raucous, but eventually the sound of a dog barking relentlessly penetrated through their talking, and Sauvage shouted to one of his companions.

'Good God, Armand! Would you go and shut up your damn stupid mutt? She's giving me a headache.'

'Are you sure it's not this cheap wine that you're giving us that's causing your headache, Sauvage?' Armand snapped as he got up. 'We all know you're keeping the good stuff under lock and key, you skinflint.'

'As though you'd know anything about wine!' Sauvage shouted after him.

As Armand left the room a strange shuddering shook the house, as though it was being dragged slowly over rocky ground.

Doors and shutters banged gently. Then there was a crash as pots fell in the kitchen that made several men jump visibly. Sauvage watched the brandy in his glass as it trembled and then sloshed, sticky and golden, against the rim. He grabbed at the edge of his table with his free hand uncertainly and glanced upwards as dust drifted down from the rafters above him.

The shaking of the earth subsided as suddenly as it had begun and as the men glanced at each other nervously, someone behind Sauvage remarked, 'Well if that was the merchant's vengeance, he might have just managed to dent one of your pans, Sauvage.'

In the quiet, Armand's dog had increased its barking, a shrill whining protest that was grating on Sauvage's nerves even more now that his companions had fallen silent.

Unsettled, he got to his feet and shouted as he headed for the door, 'Will you shut that stupid creature up, Armand!'

There was a high-pitched yelp as Armand delivered a kick to the dog, but she would not cease her barking, and as Sauvage reached the door he pushed Armand to one side and untied the rope that held the dog's collar. He gave her a kick of his own that sent her howling into the night.

'For God's sake, Sauvage!' Armand protested, 'It might take me hours to find her now.'

'She'll come back when she's ready,' Sauvage snapped back, 'come back inside, you're letting the heat out.'

'Sauvage!'

'It's not my fault your dog's an idiot.'

'No, forget her, look!'

Pierre Sauvage glanced in the direction that Armand was pointing and gave an irritable shrug, 'What is it?'

'Look at that.'

'Look at what, Armand? I don't see anything. The beach is empty.'

'Where's the sea?'

Sauvage glared at him as though he were an idiot.

'The tide's out, Armand. How drunk are you?'

'Yes,' Armand frowned, 'the tide's out, but it shouldn't be.'

'Well it obviously is out, because it's not there. What is the matter with you? Come inside, you're as stupid as your damn dog.'

'I can't see the sea, Sauvage. I've never seen it so far out before.'

'Who gives a damn, Armand? You're not a fisherman anymore, what difference does it make?'

Pierre turned to go back indoors, but Armand's strong hand on his arm restrained him.

'Sauvage …'

'What now?'

'What is that?'

Sauvage turned with a huff of exasperation and squinted towards the horizon, 'What's what? I can't see a damn thing.'

Yet there was something in Armand's voice that made him peer into the night, squinting into the darkness in annoyance.

He saw nothing. Then a low star winked out, and then another as a line of shadow slowly rose against the horizon.

'What is that?' Sauvage whispered slowly.

They stood watching in silence as the darkness rose up before them like a shroud, their brows furrowed in consternation, their minds hazy with alcohol. A breeze began to rise, bringing with it the scent of the ocean and a sound like distant thunder.

It was only when the great wave began to crest into white horses that the two men finally recognised it for what it was.

'Run,' whispered Sauvage, and they turned, glasses falling from their hands and shattering on the ground as the tsunami hurled itself towards the island.

The wall of dark water smashed down upon the land like a fist. Homes and lives were dashed to fragments with a destructive fury that tore trees up by the roots and levelled structures. Surging and boiling, the sea tore at the land, melding it with the salt and sand of the ocean floor. Then, grasping like a great claw, the churning water receded, dragging all traces of the wreckers with it, and leaving nothing but devastation in its wake.

When dawn broke the residents from further inland came at last to see what the tumultuous rage of the ocean had wrought upon the island. They were horrified to see the land so distorted; acres of forest and fertile ground had been devoured by the sea. Only a great sandy bay remained beneath the lip of higher land that was untouched. From this elevated point, they looked down onto a wasteland.

Ravens circled slowly, some alighting cautiously upon the treacherous rocks to the south of the bay where the last of the five Spanish ships had been wrecked a year ago that night.

The ocean itself was calm once again, and only the sound of a dog barking broke the silence. The sun rose in the clear sky over land that would remain infertile and covered in dunes of sand forever.

WITCHES' ROCK

Of all the girls living in the fishing village of Le Hocq, it was Madelaine who was held to be the most beautiful. This was an opinion generally put forward by the men of the village however. The women were swift to remark that Madelaine was rather too tall for a girl, and her shining black hair was a little severe against her pale skin. Her brown eyes were too dark, they pointed out, since everyone knew that blue eyes were preferable. She was far too quick-witted and opinionated to be considered truly feminine. Her cheekbones were too high; they made her look like a foreigner. She laughed too softly and her smile was too wide. She was bookish and talked about things they could not understand.

Madelaine was not, they concluded, really anything special at all and it was a tragic mystery as to why Hubert; tall, handsome, charming Hubert, should be so inconveniently in love with her.

Since childhood Hubert had been fascinated by the ghost stories and tales of fairy magic that were common throughout the island. On evenings when Madelaine was busy with her nose in a book or sewing, Hubert would go out in search of the supernatural creatures described in the legends.

'Have fun, Hu,' Madelaine murmured as she raised her book and settled deeper into her comfortable chair.

'You know, Madelaine,' Hubert said as he leant to kiss her forehead, 'if you wanted me to stay, we could curl up together and–'

'Not before the wedding, Hubert,' Madelaine said as she turned a page. 'You know that the curtains of every old biddy in the village will be twitching while they watch to see what time you leave here tonight.'

'We'll be married in two weeks! Who cares what they think?' Hubert demanded in amusement, his bright blue eyes twinkling as she deliberately ignored him.

Hubert kissed her firmly on the forehead and she blushed, waving him away as though he were a troublesome fly.

'Good night, Madelaine,' he said gently, 'I love you.'

'Yes, dear, I know,' she frowned at the page as though riveted, but failed to conceal a smile.

Hubert was laughing as the door closed behind him.

Madelaine looked up from her book.

'I love you too,' she said quietly.

❧

The evening was fair and, as Hubert walked, he considered the various legends and fables that he had sought out in many locations around the island.

He had been to the famous Ghost House of St Aubin where it was said that, on certain nights, the screams of the many men and women who had been murdered there could still be heard. Yet the ghosts remained silent upon Hubert's visits.

He had walked the hills of Bouley Bay in hopes of seeing, or even hearing, the famous giant black dog that was rumoured to roam the woods, yet somehow it remained elusive despite supposedly being the size of a bull.

In vain he searched for the Will-o'-the-Wisp-like Belengi, a creature that concealed great treasure within the marshes of St Lawrence, and would lead unwary travellers to their deaths to protect it. Hubert earned nothing from his own treasure hunt there except wet boots.

He visited the dolmens in hopes of being one of the few to see the White Lady, the Queen of the Fae, who sometimes showed herself to passers-by, but he was not one of the lucky few. The ghostly bridal procession upon the road to the millpond did not materialise on any of the nights he looked for it. No werewolves, mermaids or sirens crossed his path, no dancing goblins by the menhir stones, no crooked fairies, no spectral horses or invisible beasts, bogeymen or guardian spirits, no demon imps, devils, harpies, brownies or changelings.

In his boyhood years Hubert had even gone looking for the fairies said to bathe in the Venus Pool beneath Sorel Point, although he had not mentioned this particular adventure to Madelaine. The Venus Pool also had an older name and a darker legend, but the story was so ancient that it had been almost lost in time, as the darkest of tales often are when they are best left forgotten.

In short, there was nothing which led Hubert to believe that there was anywhere near as much magic and mystery within the forty-five square miles of Jersey as the bedtime stories of his childhood had prepared him for.

On this particular evening, beneath the full moon, Hubert's footsteps led him south along the coast towards the famous Witches' Rock, or 'Rocqueberg', as it had been known since ancient times. It was only a two-mile stroll from the village, so he had been there many times before in the hope of spotting some hideous hag in congress with the Devil. So far he had found only solitude beside the promontory of rock that jutted up from the landscape, and this evening was no different.

The rock was only a stone's throw from the beach, and had been carved by nature into exquisite beauty. It was bigger than Hubert's fisherman's cottage and formed of jagged, peach-coloured granite. In daylight the colour stood in warm, glorious contrast to the green glade surrounding it. With a sigh Hubert settled down with his back against the rock and looked out to sea, watching the moonlight dance upon the waves.

'Black dogs and white ladies,' Hubert grumbled, 'a load of damn nonsense.'

The legend surrounding Witches' Rock was an old one. The story went that on stormy days fishing boats returning to port would be hailed from the rock by witches. The witches would threaten them, saying that if the fishermen did not throw them the thirteenth fish of their catch, they would raise the storm and dash the fishing boats against the rocks. Men who refused would lose their vessel, and sometimes their lives, to the storm. But on one such occasion the demanding witches had been defied by the captain of a fishing vessel. He had lifted a starfish from his net and cut one of its five arms away before throwing this makeshift symbol of the holy cross at their feet. The witches had screamed and disappeared, and the storm had subsided at once.

The last time he had visited Witches' Rock, Hubert had told Madelaine of the legend.

'Poor starfish,' she had remarked calmly. 'Starfish aren't even really fish, you know. Besides, there must be easier ways to make a cross. Why didn't the fishermen just take one with them?'

'I have my crucifix,' Hubert had remarked, touching the tiny golden cross that he always wore at his throat, 'so you don't need to worry.'

'I am certain I don't,' Madelaine reassured him with a wry smile.

'You never know,' Hubert said, slightly defensive, 'I may run across something supernatural one day. I heard a dog howl in Bouley Bay once.'

'I don't doubt that you heard a dog howl, Hu,' Madelaine said gently, 'I just think it's unlikely that it was a giant spectral hound come to herald a storm.'

'I know,' Hubert grinned, 'it sounded more like the tavern's mongrel.'

'Never mind, darling,' Madelaine laughed, giving him a swift hug. 'Give it time. Magical things are always more likely to occur during a full moon anyway.'

'Do you really think so?'

'Not really, love. Take a coat won't you?'

'You could come, you know,' he had pointed out as she walked him out of her house and stood above him upon the steps.

'When we're married,' she had told him firmly.

'Don't you trust me?' he'd asked her, raising one eyebrow.

'Perhaps I don't trust myself,' she had laughed and, before he could formulate a response, she had quickly shut the door.

The memory brought a grin to his face and a smile was still lingering about his lips as he fell asleep against the cool stone.

He was awoken, disoriented, by a soft light and the sound of a woman's laughter. He felt confused, as though he had been drinking. His arms were slightly numb.

'Madelaine?' he asked as he sat up and passed a hand over his eyes.

It was still night. The glow seemed to emanate from the great rock itself and in the gentle light four lovely women spun and danced with the grace of ballerinas, their laughter sweet as the bubbling of fresh springs. The song they sang was haunting, filled with both sadness and exaltation.

Hubert thought he knew all of the local young people, but the women were unfamiliar to him. He would certainly have noticed if he had seen any of them before. They were possessed of ethereal beauty. One, dressed all in green, had rich chestnut curls, tanned skin and deep brown eyes. Another, wearing a delicate blue dress, had flowing hair as silvery white as the breaking of waves and eyes as green as the depths of the sea. A girl dressed all in red had a flame-coloured fall of hair and eyes of a soft, smoky grey smouldering in a way that brought colour to Hubert's cheeks.

The loveliest of them though, to Hubert's eyes at least, had a mass of golden curls and cornflower blue eyes and was wearing a diaphanous white gown which barely concealed the slender curves of her body as she danced.

Feeling suddenly unpleasantly voyeuristic, Hubert cleared his throat and called out a friendly, 'Hello?'

He moved out from where he rested so that he could be more easily seen in case they had not noticed him, stumbling as he stood. Their smiles and laughter revealed that they had been aware of him as they danced over.

'Were you dreaming sweet dreams, handsome man?'

'Did we wake you?'

'What brings you to our rock on this fair night?'

'What is your name?'

Their flurry of questions and the touch of their fingers upon his arms as each tried to catch his attention made him laugh awkwardly.

'My name is Hubert, and I came looking for witches and fell asleep waiting. Silly of me, I suppose, but I have always been interested in magic and I never seem to find any. I am glad that you woke me though. I'm a fisherman so I'll need to be ready to sail with the tide in the morning.'

'Not tomorrow, no!' the silver-haired woman said earnestly.

'Do not sail tomorrow,' the golden-haired girl agreed and her voice was soft and powerful. 'There will be a great storm. Stay away from the sea.' The two exchanged glances and nodded in firm agreement.

'If you say so,' said Hubert with a smile. He was certain the weather would be good, but he had no wish to argue with them.

'Oh we do, we do say so,' they laughed and the silver-haired girl spun and danced. 'The waves will be as high as hills and unwary sailors will be driven onto the rocks. Stay away from the ocean tomorrow, sweet Hubert.'

'The wind will rise and howl, the air itself will be a force strong enough to lay a man off of his feet,' his golden-haired favourite smiled into his eyes, 'it will be glorious.'

She seemed so delighted that he couldn't help but laugh with her.

'What is your name?' he asked her as the other women danced and spun, their clothing lifting with their grace like gossamer upon the breeze, a whirl of colour and sound.

'My name?' The girl frowned as though it took her a moment to recall. 'My name is Sookie Gaudain,' she said thoughtfully, and a shadow seemed to pass over her face for an instant.

'That is the sweetest name I ever heard,' Hubert said and then shook his head to clear it, 'or second sweetest, perhaps. I am to be married in two weeks,' he added.

This fact, that had been so delightful to him a few hours before, now seemed something of an inconvenient annoyance.

'Married?' Sookie's disappointment was glorious to behold. 'But Hubert, I have only just found you.'

She leaned on his chest and looked beseechingly into his eyes.

It was as though he were still half asleep and he could not quite focus his eyes upon her. She seemed to glow from within. The longer he looked at her, the more gorgeous she became. It was as though, in staring at her, he realised that every feature was the epitome of feminine perfection. The other girls seemed almost insubstantial now compared to her, and they danced and whirled at a slight remove.

'Madelaine would be upset if she were even to see me talking to you like this …' Hubert shook his head again as he tried to picture Madelaine's face, 'I have made promises. She would probably …' he frowned slightly. Thinking was difficult, as though his mind was filled with sweet syrup.

'She might even put her damn book down for a moment. I should go, Sookie. I love her and she loves me. Well, I *think* she does. I must go.'

He stepped away from her, working hard not to stumble and fall.

'She cannot possibly love you as I do, Hubert,' Sookie's voice was almost a song, rising and falling with those of the other women. 'Say that you will think of me,' she begged, her voice was a symphony in his ears and he knew he could refuse her nothing.

'Say that you will visit me here tomorrow, at midnight. I will give you a gift, something truly magical that will prove me worthy of your love. Give me a chance. Say that I mean that much to you, Hubert. Two things I ask of you in return for my love. Promise me that you will come, and promise that you will not sail tomorrow.'

'I promise,' Hubert whispered, and while he still could, he turned and strode away, his footsteps uncertain.

'Stay away from the sea at the turning of the tide!' she called after him, her voice was a command.

He woke feeling groggy and confused. There were four shallow cuts upon his arms but he didn't remember injuring himself. Perhaps he had stumbled through a gorse bush on his way home. He didn't remember much of his return journey, haunted as he had been by the image of the girl with the golden hair dancing before his eyes and the sound of her soft voice echoing in his ears.

The sunlight streamed through his window and a glance at the clock had him swearing and struggling into his clothes. His fingers were awkward and numb. He felt strange and he had to lean against the wall to pull on his boots.

He was almost out of the door before he remembered his promise to Sookie. The sky was blue, scattered with small clouds moving at leisure upon a gentle wind. A perfect day to put to sea. A promise was a promise, however, and with a sigh Hubert kicked off his boots again and smiled. He would laugh at her prediction of a storm when he saw her that night. Beautiful they might be, but dancing women did not know the weather like a fisherman born and bred. How long had it been since he had taken a day away from his work? He had toiled every available hour to find money for the wedding. Madelaine had been orphaned and lived on the edge of poverty in the tiny run-down cottage that had belonged to her father. She took in small mending jobs, kept a few hens and sold the eggs. Then his thoughts of Madelaine slipped from his mind like errant quicksilver. Hubert wondered how and where Sookie lived.

He was lost in a sleepy reverie of Sookie and her companions when he was startled into wakefulness by a sharp rap at the door. Four swift knocks. *Madelaine.*

A slight sense of unease stirred within him. Had he done anything wrong last night? Anything worthy of guilt? The thought filled him with annoyance, and he frowned as he stumbled over and opened the door to her. How could anything related to Sookie Gaudain possibly be wrong?

Madelaine smiled up into his eyes with relief.

'Oh Hu, you are here! When I saw your boat in the harbour I thought some harm may have befallen you last night. Are you well? You look awful,' she added, pulling a face, 'do you need anything, my love?'

'No, thank you, Madelaine. I just … I had a bit of an adventure last night, and I don't know why but …'

'What happened to your arms, Hu? You're all cut up and …' she leaned to the side and frowned at the side of his head, 'There's a chunk missing out of your hair. Several chunks actually. What *have* you been doing?'

'What? Oh I don't know,' Hubert scratched at his hair. 'Maybe I fell over on the way home last night. I was confused.'

'Confused by what? Hubert what's wrong with you? Your eyes look strange. You're not *drunk* are you, Hu?'

'No I'm not drunk,' Hubert said indignantly, 'it's first thing in the morning.'

'Hubert it's past noon! All the other fishermen have been out for hours. What adventure did you have?'

'Well I went to the rock, and there were no witches there, but there were these girls there instead, Madelaine …' Hubert slid his back slowly down the doorframe and sat on the step.

'Girls, Hubert?' Madelaine's face was unreadable.

'Four ladies, dancing. You should have seen them! They were like angels, and the singing, Madelaine, it was incredible. It was like nothing I've ever heard, it was haunting, it was …' he waved his hands vaguely.

'Magical?' Madelaine suggested carefully.

'Yes, *magical* … they were so beautiful … the most beautiful girls I've ever seen …'

Hubert gazed off into middle distance, as images of the women danced before his hazy gaze. His eyes began to close.

Madelaine's right eyebrow climbed slowly into an arch until her face was a mask of quiet, wrathful enquiry.

'The *most* beautiful?' she asked with dangerous calm.

'One of them in particular,' Hubert mumbled, 'you can't imagine how gorgeous she was …'

'I'm sure I can't,' Madelaine said coldly, 'and you spoke to these women did you?'

'Yes, of course. I fell asleep, but when I woke up and I saw them dancing in the light from the rock, I called out to them and we spoke. Well, I spoke mostly to Sookie Gaudain, I suppose …'

'*Sookie?*' Madelaine's face was a mask of horror

'Yes, why? Do you know her?' Hubert asked eagerly.

'No, it's just the most ridiculous name I've ever heard,' Madelaine gave a gasp of laughter, and then gathered herself. 'Did you have the cuts on your arms and hair missing when you woke up last night, Hubert?'

'Good Lord, I can't remember! What difference does it make?'

Madelaine composed herself and tucked her hair behind her ears as a rising wind began to blow it around her face.

'Did you recognise these women, Hu? Have you ever seen any of these amazingly beautiful women with their magical singing and dancing before last night?'

'No, none of them.'

'Right then,' Madelaine put her hand out to test the temperature of his forehead and he jerked back irritably.

'I'm not ill,' he grumbled.

'No, not ill, darling,' Madelaine said gently. 'Well then, Hu, I think it might be better if you were to stay away from the Witches' Rock in future. Will you do that for me, my love? Will you promise?'

'What? No, Madelaine! I'm going back tonight. I made a promise to Sookie that I would. I am to meet her no later than midnight.'

Madelaine's mouth moved in astonishment, but for a moment no words came out. Then she said loudly, 'Are you insane, Hubert? You can't go back there! Those women are witches!'

'What?' Hubert looked at her like she was an idiot, 'Don't be absurd!'

'Magical singing? Dancing around the Witches' Rock? You with blood and hair missing, sitting here in a daze, half-asleep in the middle of the day! You look like a half-sheared sheep and you just told your own fiancé that you met the most beautiful women you've ever seen! Are you demented, Hubert? A meeting at midnight? Well no,' she remarked sarcastically, 'that doesn't sound spooky or evil *at all*. You are *not* going back to that stupid rock tonight. I forbid you!'

'Don't be ridiculous, Madelaine,' Hubert put his hand out to catch the first drops of rain that were beginning to fall as the clouds closed in. 'Those women were closer to goddesses than witches. Besides, I made a promise! I intend to keep it. Who are you to forbid me anything anyway?'

'I am your wife! Or I will be if you snap out of this stupor and get a hair cut. You've made promises to me too, Hubert. What of those?'

'I don't know, Madelaine,' Hubert said, his blue eyes black and unfocused, 'would you even care if I did break them? Would you stop reading for long enough to notice? At least I know that Sookie loves me. When it comes to you, I never know what you're thinking. Sometimes I think you'd be just as happy without me.'

Madelaine's mouth had dropped open in astonishment.

'I agreed to marry you, Hubert,' she said, two high spots of colour forming on her pale cheekbones, 'does that not indicate a certain degree of affection?'

'Affection?' Hubert laughed, 'Is that what you're offering me, Madelaine? *Affection*? Sookie loves me passionately!'

'Oh does she, Hubert?' Madelaine snarled. 'And what could *possibly* have happened last night to make you think that?'

'She said so!'

'Dear God, you are *such* a fool!'

'Maybe I am a fool!' Hubert shouted, stumbling to his feet. 'After all, I've been planning to marry a woman who can only offer me *affection*, who barely lets me touch her and who'd rather spend her time with her nose stuck in a book or knitting socks than with her own damn fiancé! Now that I know what real love feels like, I wonder if you even care for me at all!'

Madelaine took a shaky step backwards and clasped her hands at her waist. The rain was falling steadily now, heavy drops that soaked her gown and plastered her hair to her head. Thunder rumbled ominously from off the coast and Hubert suddenly looked seawards with an odd little smile.

'That's not fair, Hubert,' Madelaine said huskily, 'you know that isn't how I meant it. You know how the gossips in this village are. I have to protect myself from scandal. I don't have anyone except you, and now you're …' her red lips twisted as though she would cry but then she shook her head violently.

Straightening her dress firmly she looked him in the eyes. 'Well there's no point talking to you when you're like this. You're obviously bewitched or under a spell so I think–'

'You believe that if it makes you feel better, Madelaine,' Hubert said coldly. 'Sookie said there would be a storm. It seems she's wise as well as beautiful. You should go home, you're getting wet.'

He stepped back inside and shut the door on her.

Madelaine walked back to her house through the pouring rain. The wind was rising and whipping her raven hair around her face and into her eyes.

She found it hard to breathe for the tightness in her chest. Was this witchcraft? Or had Hubert simply found somebody he preferred? Tears mixed with rain upon her cheeks and she wiped the moisture away impatiently. The wind buffeted her, causing her to stumble. There was a strange sound upon the rising tempest, a song upon the wind, and briefly Madelaine wondered at how the storm had risen so quickly. The men at sea would be hauling in their nets as swiftly as they could. At least Hubert was safe at home. For now anyway.

She unlocked her front door, the key shaking in her hands and tears blurring her vision. Her humble cottage creaked with the rising storm and the wind whistled in the empty fireplace. Composing herself, Madelaine sunk into a chair at her little kitchen table and for a very long time she simply sat. Her clothes were damp and her teeth worried at her lower lip as the storm gathered strength outside. The rain drummed like angry fingers upon her window.

She toyed with the binding of the latest book that she had borrowed from one of the older ladies in the village. It was the third volume of a gothic novel by Ann Radcliffe, published only a few years before. Madelaine found it to be quite dreadful, yet she had been enjoying it immensely. She knew that she would not be able to concentrate upon it now. Her encounter with Hubert had left her agitated and afraid.

At last she realised that the gathering darkness outside was not only the heavy rain clouds. The afternoon was turning to evening as she sat and fretted. She stirred and blinked, then making a decision, she stood and headed back to the door.

Madelaine hesitated on her doorstep, listening to the wailing wind, watching the rain beat against the ground. Then she swore quietly and, walking swiftly and with great determination, she turned her footsteps towards the parish church of St Clement.

She was soaked through by the time she got there, and when she opened the door of the church the wind caught it and slammed it hard open against the wall inside, causing the Reverend Bromley Le Couteur to jump visibly.

'Reverend, Sir,' Madelaine called as she strode towards him, 'what do you know about witchcraft? I'm sure I've heard you mention it in a few of your sermons.'

'Ah, Madelaine,' Reverend Le Couteur smoothed his hair and composed himself, 'and I thought you weren't paying attention. You're always knitting and what-not.'

'The Devil makes work for idle hands, Reverend,' Madelaine said with an apologetic smile as she looked down into his eyes from her superior height. 'If a woman thought her fiancé might be under a spell, what might she do about that?'

'Pardon me, Madelaine?'

'It's Hubert. I think he's under a spell. Either that or he's suddenly become horrible and cruel and … I'm trying to give him the benefit of the doubt.'

The Reverend chuckled quietly, 'Oh, Madelaine, whatever's going on, I'm sure he's just pulling your leg. You know he loves all that mystical nonsense. He's always asking me about witches and demons and all such things.'

'No, Reverend Le Couteur,' Madelaine paused to wring her hair out, drops of water splattering onto the floor next to those slowly dripping from her sodden clothing, 'I wouldn't have come out in this if Hubert were playing a game. He saw women singing and dancing at the Witches' Rock last night, and now he's dazed and has cuts on his arms. He's talking like he might call off our wedding over some girl he met there called Sookie Gaudain and I'll be damned–'

'Sookie Gaudain?' The Reverend's voice was sharp.

'Yes, that's what he called her. Do you know the name?'

'It's not one I'd be likely to forget in this lifetime but …'

'Please tell me who she is, if you know, Reverend.'

Bromley Le Couteur wrapped his arms around his Bible and hugged it to his chest almost unconsciously, as a child might hug a teddy bear.

'It's not possible that he met the same girl that I know of. Sookie Gaudain was murdered. On the rocks by the harbour during a great storm. This was when I was just a boy. She was … hurt in the way that men sometimes hurt women. The village was in shock. I am sorry, Madelaine. Such things should not be talked of perhaps. Or maybe they should never be forgotten. I was too young to remember her well, but they say she was a sweet girl, very quiet and kind. This woman may be some relative of hers perhaps?'

Madelaine bit her lip and shivered with cold and horror.

'Did they find who did it?' she asked quietly. 'Was he punished? Was he hanged?'

The Reverend shook his head slowly, 'No but … in the weeks that followed four men were found dead also. Young men from along the coast, and they had … well it's not the sort of thing one should say to a young lady of your–'

'Reverend, Sir, please! I am not a child. *Tell* me.'

'They were, well, they were mutilated, Madelaine. Cut into, the same words over and over again *"My name is Sookie Gaudain"*.'

'Dear God,' Madelaine stared at him in horror. 'Oh Reverend, please think of something I can use to rid Hubert of this spell before he gets himself killed!'

'It can't be her, Madelaine, it simply can't–'

'Well let's not take the risk just in case,' Madelaine said firmly. 'Now, if they are spirits or witches, what do I need? Holy water? Scripture? Do you need to perform an exorcism?'

Reverend Le Couteur walked to the wall of the church and unhooked a large cross, about the size of his forearm, and returned to her with it.

'If you could simply make Hubert hold this cross–'

'I don't think that will work, Reverend. Hubert already wears a little golden cross on a necklace that his mother gave him. He was wearing it when I saw him earlier. He never takes it off.'

'Ah ... yes! But this cross is silver. Silver is known to be anathema to supernatural creatures.'

'So it's the silver, not the *cross* that matters?' Madelaine nodded and then spoke slowly: 'So what you're telling me, is that this holy cross is of no more use in this matter than the silver teaspoon that my grandmother gave to me for my fourth birthday? I could use a *spoon* to fight the forces of evil?'

The Reverend looked slightly uncomfortable and shrugged, 'Well, my mother always said that in dealing with the supernatural, one should use cold steel and silver. The symbol of our Lord certainly can't do any harm. Shall I come with you to his home?' he offered.

'Why, Reverend?'

'To pray for him, perhaps?'

'Oh Reverend! You can do that in here without getting soaked to the skin. Besides,' Madelaine lifted her eyes to the heavens as she listened to the howl of the wind, 'I think some of your other parishioners will be seeking you out very soon. The men are all trapped at sea and their families will be looking to you for comfort if they don't return soon. I will take the cross though, Reverend, if you don't mind. It looks like it has a nice heft to it if I need to knock Hubert out to make him stay at home.'

'It's from the fifteenth century, Madelaine,' Bromley Le Couteur said carefully, 'Very valuable and–'

'Hubert is valuable too, Reverend, Sir. Don't worry, I won't dent it and I'll get it back to you just as soon as I can. Thank you so much for your guidance, and for trusting me with this.'

Madelaine took the ornate cross in her delicate hands and swung it experimentally as though it was a cricket bat.

'Nice,' she muttered, and stalked from the church back out into the raging storm to hurry towards the village.

Her banging at Hubert's door was in vain, however. He had already departed.

The wind howled, a voice of rage and pain and vengeance, yet doors stood open in the village, as wives and mothers looked seaward with faces of dread.

Madelaine's hair whipped about her face, blinding her as she shivered in the storm.

'Has anyone seen Hubert?' she called out to the women huddled in doorways and under eaves.

Their faces were pale under their tans, and they shook their heads in the negative.

'He's not at sea, Madelaine. He went walking off along the shore,' Mrs Le Sauteur called, trying to reassure her.

'Damn it,' Madelaine said harshly, tears starting in her eyes.

She was about to set off, then her sensible nature asserted itself. Instead she returned to her little cottage. Quickly she changed into dry, light clothes and tied back her hair. She threw on an oilskin to keep out the rain, and kicked off her small, sodden shoes in favour of thick socks and sturdy boots. She regarded herself with a grim smile in her little mirror. As far as confronting her competition for Hubert's heart, she was certainly not looking her best. But practicality had always been more in her nature than vanity. She quickly found her precious silver teaspoon and slipped it into her pocket. Grabbing up the silver cross once again, she returned into the storm with a steady stride. And then, because the panic that had been rising in her chest refused to be suppressed any longer, she began to run.

The wind and rain buffeted her violently as she made her way swiftly along the coast, roaring in her ears and blinding her eyes. She might have passed within only a few feet of Hubert or run straight into him, so limited was her vision.

For two long miles she fought the power of the storm, wind dragging at her clothes and rain forcing its way down her neck and into her boots as the light faded to a purple sunset of ragged clouds. Darkness crawled across the land behind her.

When she saw a soft glow ahead of her, she thought for a moment that it was the sunset. Then, as she moved into the eye of the storm where the wind dropped suddenly and the rain fell more gently, she saw the Witches' Rock. It was luminous and warm with soft light and the reflecting glow of a roaring fire. She gripped at the heavy cross in her arms and stopped dead in her tracks.

Hubert sat with a vacant smile upon his face as he spoke, too soft for Madelaine to hear the words, but with each exhalation it was as though some light emerged with his breath. The creature that floated before him like a white spectre seemed to be drawing it from his lungs into her own.

Madelaine blinked and tried to focus on the woman, but it was as though her eyes could only begin to comprehend one aspect of the creature before they saw the beginnings of another. The witch was a gorgeous beauty in the glamour of her power, a creature of light and air, but somehow in glimpses and moments she had the face of a dead woman, bloodied and bruised.

Other figures moved nearby. Madelaine gasped as she realised that the flames of the dancing fire were twisted into the shape of a woman in red. Her skin appeared to boil and blister, then it smoothed flawlessly in an endless cycle as she looked first burned, then glorious. Hunkered nearby, just out of reach of this elemental beauty, was a figure which seemed at first like an olive-skinned girl, then twisted before Madelaine's eyes into a woman crafted of wizened roots as she flowed across the ground with the sinister crawl of ivy. A woman dressed in blue floated like a serene and flawless corpse, her white hair stirred and floated as though moved by gentle waves in the depths of the ocean. Of them all, Madelaine found this elemental creature of water to be the most beautiful and the most fascinating. Despite her desire to reach Hubert, Madelaine could hardly stand to look away from her. She began to understand the force of Hubert's enchantment.

'Hubert!' Madelaine's voice cracked with panic as she forced herself to walk towards these strange apparitions.

'Madelaine?' Hubert's voice was tired and slightly irritated as he turned to her, 'What are you doing here?'

'I've come to take you home, Hubert. You have to leave with me. It isn't safe here.'

The witches smiled and began to laugh gently.

'Don't be silly, Madelaine,' Hubert said in exasperation, 'this is Sookie. They aren't witches. Look at them. How could such sweet and beautiful women be dangerous?'

'We are creatures of nature,' whispered the floating corpse in blue, as though she knew that Madelaine's eyes kept creeping back to her. 'The fire, the earth, the wind and the ocean. Don't you wish to be our friends? We can give you fair winds and calm seas, money and power, in exchange for so little … A few drops of blood, the breath from your lungs … Nothing you need …'

'Thank you very kindly, madam,' Madelaine said with a shaky curtsy, 'but I rather think we might just go home, if it's all the same to you.'

'Madelaine, don't be so rude,' Hubert mumbled, turning his bewitched smile back to the floating apparition before him, 'you don't need that crucifix. I didn't realise that you were so religious.'

'You're quite right, Hu,' Madelaine said with forced calm as she walked up to him, 'it was very silly of me to bring it. Here, why don't you hold it for me? It's a bit heavy and Reverend Le Couteur says it's very valuable. He's such a nice man, I wouldn't want to drop it.'

Hubert reached out his hand and took the cross from her impatiently. The second it left Madelaine's grasp her eyes saw exactly what Hubert had been seeing. Four gorgeous woman, their feet on the ground, their eyes kind and their smiles warm. The woman in white frowned slightly as Hubert suddenly gasped and fell back-wards away from her, scrambling to Madelaine's feet and standing protectively before her, grasping the cross like a weapon.

'Silver?' Sookie Gaudain asked with a sigh.

'This one is mine,' the woman in blue said gently as she stepped forward, waving Sookie aside impatiently. She was glorious. Her voice caressed and her eyes enchanted as she spoke.

'You lost your parents to the sea, didn't you Madelaine? You look out sometimes and wonder … Will it take you too one day? Will it take the man you love? You know it would be so peaceful down there, in the cool and in the deep. I could take you with me into the embrace of the ocean, and you could …'

Madelaine slipped her hand into her pocket and gripped her silver spoon. The enchanting whisper that so tempted her was just a voice once more.

'Hubert,' the floating spectre of Sookie Gaudain reached out to him sadly, 'do you not love me anymore? You who so love the wind in your sails and upon your skin?'

'I'm afraid he's already taken,' Madelaine said firmly, 'I know what happened to you, Sookie, and I am sorry, but I don't under-stand how you came to be like this.'

'I died a violent death,' Sookie's form frayed and billowed like silk in a strong wind as she spoke. 'At the moment of my passing something crept in from the storm. A thing of nature and of rage … and then I became … *something more.*'

'I was drowned by my lover,' the floating corpse in blue dipped her head and somersaulted with slow grace as though she were turning under the water. 'The fool should never have gone back to sea. I was waiting for him in the waves.'

'I was murdered by my husband and buried beneath the roots of a tree,' whispered the woman in green, crawling forward. 'He did not have time to marry his lover, as he had planned to do after my death. I dragged him down into the earth and choked him with my roots.'

'*Burned!*' the redhead threw back her head and laughed a roar of flame. 'Burned as a witch by my cruel, lying brothers. Such a glorious irony! Innocent I burned … *then* I became a witch …' She whirled and whispered and clenched a flaming fist, '*Then they all burned.*'

'I see,' said Madelaine matter-of-factly, her voice trembling, 'then I'm sure they all had it coming, and I am sorry for you all. But my Hubert is a good man, and he wouldn't hurt a fly … well,' Madelaine allowed, 'fish perhaps. Lots of fish, but he would certainly never harm a woman. He isn't a monster. He's kind and honest … a trifle slow occasionally,' she said sharply, shooting him a glare that made him wince, 'but he's a decent man. How many decent men have you tried to kill in this storm tonight? How many good men have you killed down the years?'

'Never enough … Never enough …' Sookie muttered. 'The wind will howl, the sails will tear.'

'A fire in the rigging.'

'Waves to drive them onto the rocks.'

'The wooden hulls will split, the wooden masts will rot.'

Their voices joined and merged and raised into the song of the storm.

Hubert was drawing Madelaine away slowly with the cross held before him. 'Take the cross, Madelaine,' he said, 'please, I need you to be safe.'

'It's fine Hu, I have a spoon,' she held it up for him to see and he stared at it in confusion.

'There will be other times, other storms. We have all the time in the world,' Sookie smiled a corpse's smile.

'Farewell to you sweet children. Should you ever wish to join us …'

The water-witch stared longingly into Madelaine's eyes, and she felt something ache deep within her.

'Thank you. We'll know where to find you,' Madelaine said politely.

Taking Hubert's hand in her own she walked swiftly from the circle of light and back out into the raging storm. The rain against her face was like a slap that shook her from her brave calm and suddenly she was shaking and running.

Hubert kept pace with her easily.

'Why didn't they kill me?' he asked. 'Why didn't they let me go out in the storm and try to kill me with the others?'

'Well you are quite loveable.' Madelaine stumbled and he caught her. 'Anyway, I rather suspect that, with their hatred of men who betray women, had you wavered in your loyalty to me, they were waiting to tear you to pieces. Perhaps I'm wrong.'

'The storm is dying a little. Do you think they listened to you when you talked about the villagers being good men?'

'No, I think they were using whatever they were taking from you to power their magic and now it's gone. How do you feel?'

'Like I could eat a horse and sleep for a week. I have a vicious headache, but other than that I'm not too bad.'

The storm lessened a little as they made their way back along the coast to the village. By the time they arrived at Madelaine's door, the wind had fallen to a mournful howl. They were both soaked to the skin, but the rain was no longer blinding.

'I should let you get dry then,' Hubert said, gripping her hands tightly, 'I'll leave you to get some–'

'Nonsense,' Madelaine interrupted him firmly, 'I'm not letting you out of my sight. You may sleep in my chair tonight, but so help me, Hubert, if you so much as mention Sookie Gaudain or tell me that she's beautiful I shall smack you with this enormous cross.'

'No, no, of course not,' Hubert said, cringing in embarrassment as Madelaine forced the door open and they stumbled in from the storm. 'If I could just have a towel, and a blanket, I promise I'll go right to sleep.'

Sleep found neither of them that night however. They listened to the wind whisper and moan, and then settle. They talked softly until dawn of magic and mysteries.

Madelaine surprised Hubert while she was making breakfast by bursting into violent tears and sobbing wildly against his chest for several minutes before clearing her throat, blowing her nose loudly and then saying, 'Well that was embarrassing.'

'I'm so sorry, Madelaine, my love,' Hubert said, drawing her back into his arms, 'I promise I won't ever go looking for magic again.'

He sounded so sad that Madelaine gave a snort of laughter.

'Oh, Hu, you'd be miserable without your adventures, and you know it. Especially now that you know they aren't just a complete waste of time. However, I think in future I had better come with you,' she laughed shakily, 'I have a spoon you know.'

'I would feel so much safer with you to protect me,' he said with mock solemnity.

'Yes, and whenever it turns out to be a wild goose chase, then we can find other ways to pass the time.'

Hubert kissed her softly and she fluttered her hands at him, blushing, 'Get away from me you awful man, my eggs are starting to burn.'

Hubert grinned and gently tucked her hair behind her ear.

'Behave yourself or you won't get any breakfast at all!' Madelaine exclaimed, 'Go and sit down. You were telling me a story before I fell into hysterics. What was it? Tell me about this legend of Bonne Nuit Bay before I die of embarrassment.'

Hubert sat down, laughing, 'The tale of the Kelpie? Yes certainly. Where was I?'

And as he began to pour the tea, Hubert told Madelaine the legend of the Water Horse.

THE WATER HORSE

The errant breeze lifted and whipped Anne-Marie's dark curls, blowing them about her face as she walked alone beside the sea. Waves crashed against the stony shore and glittered in the pale moonlight. She tasted sea-spray on her lips and turned her face to the ocean, losing herself in the rhythm of the waves as she thought of William.

Before William had left for the war, he and Anne-Marie would walk here together around the curve of Bonne Nuit Bay, talking of how they would be married and the home that they would make together. They spoke of planting an orchard so that William could make and sell cider. Anne-Marie would bake apple pies and churn black butter to sell in the village of St John.

The night before he had departed William had placed a ring of silver upon her finger, for he could not afford gold, and begged her to wait for him. Now when Anne-Marie could not sleep for worrying that William might be killed in the fighting, she would walk along the bay in the darkness. Sometimes she would simply stand looking out across the ocean in the faint hope that she might see his ship, homeward bound upon the horizon.

Some of the other girls with husbands or sweethearts away to war would sometimes skim stones on the water. For each time the stone skipped across the surface, they said, they would count it as another month to wait for the return of their lovers from battle. Anne-Marie had often watched in amusement as girls she knew to be experts in skipping stones threw lazy, half-hearted casts, which only touched the water once or twice before sinking beneath. While she was not superstitious or fanciful herself, on this particular evening Anne-Marie began idly skipping pebbles across the flat water between the rising waves as she thought of William so far away.

'How long until you return to me, my William?' she whispered. She flicked her wrist and sent a stone skimming, but it disappeared beneath the surface without a ripple. Anne-Marie blinked and pushed her wind-swept hair back from her forehead. Before she could bend to pick up another pebble, a pale hand clutching the stone which she had cast broke the surface of the water. Then a man, the image of William, rose dripping from beneath the waves, water pouring from his dark hair and over his bare shoulders. Anne-Marie stifled a cry of alarm. Was this her William? Or was it his ghost, come to tell her of his death?

She stepped closer into the shallows, heedless of the cold water lapping at her ankles and soaking into her dress. Every detail of William's dripping features was exactly as she remembered. His eyes though … William's eyes were the bright blue of a summer sky. The eyes of this man were as black as the depths of the ocean.

'William?' she whispered, her voice quavering with uncertainty as she stepped into the waves, 'Will, is that you? Are you alright?'

She waded in deeper, reached out her hand to him and his fingers clamped around her wrist with a grip as cold as the icy waves which crashed around them.

'Come be my bride,' hissed the creature and Anne-Marie tried to pull away from this thing that looked so much like her betrothed. The fingers, which dug into her wrist, turned to claws, the pale skin to scales, and Anne-Marie cried out in horror as she watched William's beloved face distort and shift into the face of a demon. She was being dragged further from shore, her feet slipping on the shifting stones and sand. The demon, which had looked so much like William, bared his fangs in a snarl as she fought him. With all her strength Anne-Marie could not shake his grip, and for all her struggles she could not break free from him. The waves were up to her chest and water splashed into her eyes. Desperately she tried to pry the claws from her right wrist with her free hand. As the silver ring on her left ring finger touched the cold flesh of the creature, the demon roared as though it had been burned and released her.

Anne-Marie struggled back through the churning surf, her long skirts dragging in the water and holding her back as though hands clutched at the hem. She ran free of the water and up the beach, not daring to look back. She ran until her feet struck the dark earth of the hill to her home. She could not catch her breath and her legs trembled. When she reached her house she slammed and barred the door behind her, faint with exhaustion and fear, threw off her clothes and huddled shivering under the bedclothes.

When Anne-Marie woke in the pale light of dawn, she wondered, in the haze of awakening, whether it had been a terrible nightmare. Then she noticed her soaked and sandy clothing on the floor where she had dropped it the night before.

Confused and terrified, Anne-Marie told no one of the night's events, concerned that they would think that she had been driven mad with heartache for William. However, she did not return to the shore of Bonne Nuit Bay again. Instead she read all she could find regarding the dark demons and fairies of the sea. While she was not certain what manner of monster she had faced, she learnt that the touch of silver and mistletoe were anathema to such creatures and

would guard against their evil. She twisted her silver ring around her finger and whispered her thanks to William for the loving gift that had saved her life.

William returned from the wars thinner and paler but still very much the man she loved. Emboldened by his company and reassured by his promises to keep her safe, Anne-Marie walked with her lover once more along the shore of Bonne Nuit Bay, her fears dissolving in the sunlight and the warmth of William's hand in hers. Her worries were swept away by the sound of his laughter, but she still thought often of his dark double and refused to swim in the sea on even the hottest of days.

William spoke of the horrors and heroism that he had seen. He wept for comrades lost in battle, as well as for his noble horse Caspian, cut down beneath him during the fighting.

'A soldier's wage is meagre enough, but if I can buy a horse and return to fight again, I will have earned enough for us to be married when I return,' William told her. 'Although I would give my right arm to have my own horse back.'

Anne-Marie gave a humourless laugh, 'Enough boys are coming home with missing limbs without you wishing yours away, Will. I adored Caspian, but I would rather you kept both your arms, my love.'

William travelled to the neighbouring parishes seeking a new horse but found only carthorses and nags affordable. Each day spent with Anne-Marie was a joy to him, so he did not seek a new steed as eagerly as he might have. More than one boat sailed without him as he made his excuses and let the days go by.

Then one evening, as he returned to his cottage from the home of Anne-Marie, he came upon a horse like none he had ever seen before. Standing calmly beneath a tree was a stallion of pure white, with eyes as black as the ocean depths. Larger, and more powerful than any horse William had ever encountered, it moved with elegance and had a mane and tail that blew pale as sea foam in the breeze. William coaxed the beautiful creature to his home and it followed him willingly into his stable. He made enquiries the next day as to whether anyone was missing such an animal, but since nobody came forward to claim the stallion, nor had heard any word of it being owned by another, William decided to keep it. He reasoned that either good fortune or some silent benefactor were to be thanked for his new mount.

The next boat would sail at the end of the day. William set to work polishing and preparing his saddle and bridle so that he would be ready to leave at the turning of the tide.

'I wish you had never found the beast,' Anne-Marie sighed, 'then you would have had to stay a few more days with me at least. What if you never return? What if that creature from my nightmares should come for me again?'

William embraced her and kissed her forehead.

'The sooner I leave, the sooner I can earn enough to return to you forever. Then we can be married and you need never fear again.'

When William saw that Anne-Marie remained troubled, he set his thoughts to how he could lessen her burden of worry. He soon remembered what she had told him of the things that guard against evil magic, and setting aside his rag and polish, William walked through the woods. Eventually he found what he sought and returned to Anne-Marie with a little time to spare before his ship departed. In his hands he held a tangle of mistletoe, which he had bound into a circlet. He placed it upon her head.

'Take this mistletoe to put your mind at ease, my superstitious beauty,' he laughed as he rearranged her dark curls. 'To protect you from any evil creatures that might try to steal you away from me while I am gone.'

Anne-Marie broke off a sprig of the mistletoe and attached it to William's shirt, 'To keep you safe too,' she told him, planting a kiss upon his lips.

'I fear that mistletoe will not protect me from a sword thrust or an arrow shaft, my darling,' he smiled.

'Wear it for me then, William,' she insisted, 'just until your ship is clear of the bay. In case that thing is still in the water.'

'For you, love, anything,' and with that William kissed and embraced her one final time, before leaving regretfully to saddle his great white horse.

Anne-Marie ran on ahead to the beach so that she might wave him away from the shore. William mounted the great white stallion and rode him down the hill towards the ship where the other waiting soldiers and their ladies were gathered. As the horse's hooves met the sand and William cantered towards his fellows, the stallion suddenly changed course and increased speed. No matter how William hauled on the reins or cursed the beast it paid him no mind, its great hooves churning sand and sea as it galloped into the waves and charged deep into the water. Deeper and deeper it forged into

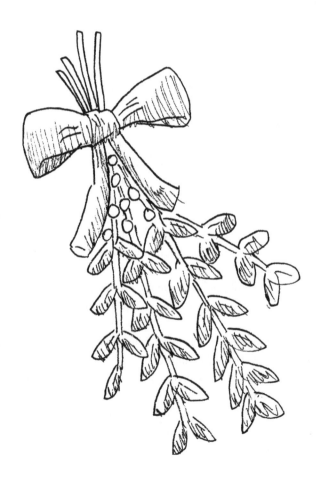

the sea, its mane and tail mixing with the foam of the waves, letting them break over its head as though it had no need for air. The water rose to William's chest and he gritted his teeth, hauling on the reins and trying in vain to pull the swimming horse's head around. It turned once and snapped at him, showing sharp, white fangs, and William realised at last that this creature was no earthly stallion. He managed to shake his feet from his stirrups and kick free of the demon creature. Turning for shore, he stuck out hard, swimming as fast and sure as only a fisherman's son can. The creature lunged and grabbed his shirt in its sharp teeth, dragging William beneath the water and shaking him like a wolf with prey.

William felt the air leave his lungs in a rush and knew he would be drowned. He thought of Anne-Marie standing on the shore and how he had laughed away her fears of monsters in the ocean, and in a sudden flash, he recalled her gift of mistletoe. With a last, desperate effort, William grasped the mistletoe that Anne-Marie had pinned to his clothing and forced it into the horse's mouth, past its fangs and deep into its throat.

The white stallion reared back and screamed a sound like nothing William had ever heard as he was thrown free. He fought to tread water, gasping for air as he tried to evade the thrashing hooves of the flailing creature. The form of the creature writhed and twisted, white hide blurring to pale flesh, and for an instant William stared into his own face, then the flesh contorted into a scaled, demonic form. It shuddered and stiffened and grew and then, with a sound like the breaking of bones, it turned to shapeless stone.

The soldiers from the shore dragged William to safety as he staggered through the breaking waves and Anne-Marie ran into his arms.

'Don't you know a Water Horse when you see one, boy?' an old soldier asked as he checked William's wounds. 'That was a kelpie you were riding, soldier. He would have dragged you down and devoured you. This whole bay is riddled with them. What were you thinking?'

'I've never heard of such a monster,' William coughed, then laughed shakily as he stroked Anne-Marie's hair and held her close saying, 'I'm sorry I ever doubted you, love.'

William eventually went to war without a horse but he returned safely to Anne-Marie having earned enough money to marry. They made a home together by the sea and from their window they could see the rock in the bay that had once been the Water Horse that had menaced them both. The locals called it Cheval Rock, and it is visible during even the highest tides, although in its warped state it bears no resemblance to the kelpie for which it is named.

While Anne-Marie and William were never troubled again by fae creatures from beneath the waves, they made sure to grow mistletoe among the trees of their orchard, and chose thereafter to walk together in the woods of an evening, rather than along the shore.

Devil's Hole

The ship, *La Josephine*, was a large red and white cutter with an incongruous devil figurehead. She was sleek and built for speed. Aaron Nedelec could imagine the grace with which she would slice through the ocean.

The owner's son, who had the unlikely name of Constant Pétibon, was fidgeting with excitement as Nedelec regarded the ship under consideration. It was a beauty, and he had to work hard to keep the excitement from his own face. To captain a ship like this was every sailor's dream.

'Not too shabby,' Nedelec said casually, 'your father has a good eye, and at that price it would be madness not to look her over. You did well to call for me.'

'That's not a new ship.'

Captain Nedelec, turning to see who had spoken, saw a gangly sailor with red hair lean beside them at the rail. The man jutted his chin at *La Josephine* and then turned to them.

'That thing washed up months back. A ghost ship. Not a soul aboard. Back then it was *The Arden*, out of Liverpool. Not that it's any of my business. Bad luck to change a ship's name though. My own name is Teller by the way.'

They shook hands.

'Well I'm not particularly superstitious, Teller,' Captain Nedelec remarked. 'It's 1851. Men should believe only what they can see with their own eyes, and I've never yet seen a ghost. The name's Aaron Nedelec,' he added as they shook hands.

'What happened to her crew?' Constant Pétibon asked, his eyes wide with youthful fascination.

The red-haired sailor shrugged, 'It's a plague ship in my opinion. Or maybe a slaver that got what it had coming. Still, they've done it up a treat, and a fresh coat of paint will do wonders.'

Aaron Nedelec gave a snort of laughter, 'How long after we walk away are you planning to make an offer on her yourself, Teller?'

'Oh not me, Captain. Got my own vessel, the *Canary Sapphire*. She's as sweet as a dream.'

Captain Nedelec grinned, 'Ah, so you're selling your boat, are you?'

'Not even for eternal youth, my friend. All I'm saying is, you can't put a price on a good boat, and that there …' again he tilted his chin at *La Josephine*, 'that's not a good boat. Heard a rumour that the shipbuilder was asked why he carved a devil for a figurehead. Do you know what he said?'

'Do tell.'

'He said he didn't carve a devil.'

Nedelec gave a derisive snort, 'Well, perhaps this Josephine, who-ever she was, was just a very ugly girl indeed.'

Teller compressed his lips without smiling and turned to leave.

'That ship is cursed, Captain,' he said over his shoulder. 'Cursed in the building. Cursed in the sailing.'

'For the price it's being sold at, the damn thing could be on fire and I'd still buy it.'

'Your choice, Nedelec. Don't say I didn't warn you though,' he raised a hand in farewell. 'Good luck to you both.'

Constant Pétibon's expression was filled with astonishment. He barely waited for the *Canary Sapphire*'s Captain to walk out of earshot before he opened his mouth to speak.

'He's pulling your leg, son,' Aaron Nedelec interrupted, 'I don't know what his angle is, but you can be sure he's got one. Just think lad; how cursed can a ship be that isn't already laying in pieces on the bottom of the ocean? She's a beauty, Pétibon. Your father has been lucky to find her.'

The Captain smiled as he looked back at the cutter. He would walk that deck and make *La Josephine* fly under his touch.

There was blood on the axe.

There was something about the way she fought the wheel, like a wild horse lunging for her head against the reins, which made her seem like a living thing. Captain Nedelec had gone over her every inch, stem to stern, and *La Josephine* was flawless. The red-haired sailor on the docks had been right about one thing, however. *La Josephine* wasn't a new ship. Two days out of port and her paint had begun to peel like a young sailor after sunburn. The red and white paint was flaking away to reveal dark wood, green trim and the edge of an old name under the new. *The Arden*, the superstitious sailor had called her. The cursive A of the old name was becoming visible, and Nedelec had to concede that there might be some truth to the tall tale, after all. The devil prow was losing its painted smile as the grim, carved visage of the wooden face beneath slowly revealed itself. Nedelec thought that the horned figurehead looked better for it. The rest of the paint should be stripped from the figurehead next time *La Josephine* was in dock, the Captain decided.

Young Pétibon was proving to be an excellent sailor and it suited Captain Nedelec to have another educated man aboard. The lad's fair hair had turned flaxen under the sun and his blue eyes shone out of a face turned tan. They played cards by candlelight when the sun slipped below the horizon, not for money, just for something to do with their hands while they talked. Sometimes the dark and dour first mate Gordon joined them, but more often it was just the Captain and the owner's son.

Constant was a good listener and had a fine combination of wit and wonder that often brought a smile to Nedelec's face. The boy's thoughtful silence one night after a long day in port at Southampton finally caused the Captain to sigh and say, 'Spit it out, Pétibon, for God's sake, whatever it is.'

Pétibon folded his cards and leaned back with a frown.

'It's nothing, Captain. I'm just having trouble sleeping. I keep having these dreams.'

'Bad dreams, Pétibon? Or have you just been away from your sweetheart too long?'

Pétibon smiled and twitched his eyebrows, 'A day is too long to be away from Nanette, but no, it's not that. I've been having nightmares. All the time. Every night, I dream that I am lost in the woods and I can't remember how I got there. I suppose you think I'm foolish?'

'Not at all,' said the Captain carefully, 'so you just dream that you are lost, is that it?'

Petitbon placed his cards upon the table and moved his expressive hands as he spoke.

'I dreamt last night that I was in the forest at the fall of dusk. I looked out into the gathering dark, and there was something moving between the trees. Something neither man nor beast. I felt that it was angry and I was afraid, so afraid that it woke me. I sound like a child, don't I?'

Nedelec shook his head reassuringly even as a line of cold fear traced down the back of his neck and lifted goosebumps on his arms. He had dreamed the same dream himself. A nightmare figure he could not make out in the shadows. Something old. Something angry. He had awoken deathly scared in a way that he had not experienced since he had been a small boy.

'It's not foolish, Pétibon,' he said steadily, 'this is your first time at sea for such a duration. It's such a change in your life. You're bound to dream of the land from time to time. I've been having strange dreams myself. They'll pass, I'm sure.'

There was blood on the axe.

The wind died on their first day out from Cherbourg. Their cargo of colza lamp oil was non-perishable and Captain Nedelec's only real niggle was that he hated to be behind schedule. A day or two spent floating on a sun-drenched sea in an unseasonably warm October would be a welcome respite for his sailors, diving and swimming off of the stern. But it would take money from his employer's pocket if it lasted.

The sea was like glass. Where the light shone upon it, it reflected as flawlessly as a mirror. Where it did not reflect the sky above Nedelec could look into the still deep as though there were no water there at all, and vertigo would twist in his stomach as his mind warned of falling from a great height into the dark and fathomless green depths below. The sun beat down with relentless strength, and eventually even Nedelec sacrificed his dignity and executed a flawless dive into the cold sea to get some respite from the baking heat. Constant Pétibon looked on with profound misery for two days before confessing that he could not swim a stroke.

'Good God, lad,' Nedelec exclaimed, 'that's neither safe nor civilized for a man at sea. You'll simply have to learn right now.'

Gordon tied a rope down from the rails so that Pétibon had something to cling to while in the water, and cling he did. Gordon stood shaking his head in profound disapproval at the boy's efforts, until Nedelec held Pétibon up by the chest like an embarrassed child and managed to coax an ungainly doggy-paddle out of him. Once he realised that he wasn't going to sink like a rock, Pétibon took to swimming with delighted enthusiasm. He often didn't clamber back aboard until his fingers were growing numb and his lips blue with the ocean chill.

Captain Nedelec was pleased to see him developing sure, strong strokes with his arms. He had grown fond of the boy and the thought that Pétibon might survive now if he was ever swept into the sea by storm or accident made the becalming seem less of a waste of their time.

The wind did not rise, however, and Nedelec found himself pacing the length of the ship like a caged animal as the third day passed. The men were bored and inclined to drink a little too much in the evenings. When sleep came it brought nightmares of being lost in the woods, lost with something watching. And there was a smell.

Nedelec's knowledge of shipbuilding and carpentry were hazy at best, but he had begun to think that perhaps there was something strange about the wood of the ship. The paint was peeling away from the hull like a snake shedding skin and the grain beneath was unusual. It was oak, he thought, but darker by far than any oak that he had seen before.

'Green wood?' Constant Pétibon suggested with an equal lack of knowledge when the Captain brought up the lingering smell over their evening card game. 'Maybe it wasn't left to dry properly? I can smell the damp of it myself. It smells like the forest.'

'She doesn't leak. I suppose that's the important thing.'

'It's like rotting leaves and hot earth, or tree sap.'

The Captain nodded. He had been thinking the same thing himself. To keep the men busy, he ordered them to scrub every inch of the ship. The sea air had the red and white paint flaking away as swiftly as gold leaf under a beggar's knife. The bare wood was mottled with strange, mouldy, green verdigris that seemed to grow back each day. Pétibon tied himself to the bowsprit above the ship's figurehead and worked with care and determination to strip the paint from the devil's torso and face without damaging the wood beneath. Paint peeled up from the contorted features like dying skin from a leprous corpse.

'Handsome devil isn't he?' Nedelec grinned from the prow.

Gordon, stood next to him, raised one dark brow and regarded the stag-horned devil with intense dislike.

'Handsome is one word for him,' Pétibon laughed, 'I'd have gone with terrifying myself. He certainly doesn't look like any Josephine I ever met.'

'That he doesn't,' the Captain agreed, 'and he's got everyone referring to my damn boat as a 'he' rather than a 'she' which is annoying. Josephine! If I had a woman that looked like that I'd never go back to shore again.'

'It is a male ship though, isn't it?' Pétibon carefully scraped at the paint around the devil's eyes. He caught a glimpse of the Captain's expression and laughed, 'I don't know, it just feels male. *The Arden ...* is that the forest from *A Midsummer Night's Dream*?'

'I never was much for the theatre,' Gordon remarked, smoothing dark hair back from his eyes.

'There's a surprise,' Captain Nedelec winked at Pétibon. 'It may have been named after the forest of Arden in England if that's where her timber is from. Although there's the Ardennes forest in France as well. Why so curious?'

'I don't know,' Pétibon wafted his hand, 'I've been too much in the sun. I feel a bit queasy to be honest.'

'Pétibon, your shoulders are burning. Why don't you take yourself for a swim,' the Captain suggested, 'this horned bastard isn't going anywhere and apparently,' he squinted at the sky, 'neither are we. You don't have any more books do you, lad? I'm bored out of my damn mind.'

There was blood on the axe.

The sickness probably started because of whatever turned the food bad. Pétibon went down first. Then men whose stomachs could not be turned by raging storms found themselves moaning like children, clutching the rails and retching themselves dry. Even the stoic Gordon took to his bunk, his tanned face paler than Captain Nedelec had ever seen it before.

The meat had gone bad overnight, although the ship's cook swore it had been the best that money could buy in Cherbourg.

'There's rot in everything,' the man complained, 'even the salt pork. The water's going stagnant as well.'

'Then boil it,' the Captain snapped, 'before we all vomit ourselves to death.'

Nedelec walked, weak with nausea, to the prow. He had hoped for fresh air, but there was still no hint of a breeze. A fog was rising off of the ocean, closing in hot and damp and confining the cloying stink of the ship until it was almost unbearable. The mist formed in slow dancing ghosts and turned the wide ocean into a white cloud that folded *The Arden* in a claustrophobic embrace.

Constant was perched on the bowsprit above the figurehead as though he was riding a horse, leaning around to look at the face of the devil. He was growing thin with sickness and his face was pale and slack.

'I think it moves sometimes. His expression,' Constant said, 'but never when I'm looking right at him.'

'You have a fever, Pétibon,' Captain Nedelec said firmly. 'Now get down before you fall off and drown. It's just an illusion, lad. It's the motion of the ocean.'

'There is no motion,' Pétibon sighed, 'we haven't moved in days. We may as well be buried in the earth. And yet the boat creaks sometimes like there's something inside trying to get out.'

'Ships creak, Pétibon, that's just what they do. You know, son, men often go stark staring mad when they're becalmed, but it usually takes more like three weeks than three days. Don't be such a goose. Come down from there before I throw you in the sea myself.'

Constant Pétibon glanced down, and then pulled himself back onto the deck with a sigh.

'I can't even see the water now. It's like we're floating in the clouds.'

'Drink some water and go to bed, Pétibon.'

'When I go below deck I feel like I'm being buried alive. Perhaps we should try to swim for land, Captain.'

'Go to bed, Pétibon!'

'Yes, Captain. Sorry, Captain.'

Pétibon's sickly steps faltered away, muffled by the mist. There was nothing to look at except the white limbo of the fog ahead and the devil of *The Arden*. The figurehead looked different now with all of the paint peeled away. He was dark wood and green mould and looked more like a forest satyr than a denizen of hell. The carving reminded Captain Nedelec of a picture that he had once seen of the forest god Pan. However this stag-horned creature, with his grim visage, did not look the type to play upon pipes or dance in the moonlight.

Nedelec's head ached and his skin was hot and cold. Leaving the becalmed ship unmanned with the sails furled, the Captain headed to his cabin to try and sleep, knowing, even as he rested his head, what dreams would come when he closed his eyes.

The fever dreams were vivid, powerful and filled with colour, they distorted time, and Nedelec was uncertain whether hours passed or days or merely minutes. It seemed as though the places in his sleep were no longer his own nightmares, but the memories of something else, something stirring in the timbers of the ship. It poisoned the air with an inescapable truth: the knowledge that there were places in the forest, very old places, where men simply should not go. It was a matter of respect. It was a matter of self-preservation.

Nedelec dreamt of a place where the trees were ancient and aware. A glade where an ancient tree was symbiotic with something older than the race of man, and far more powerful. A creature that had slept in the dark depths of the forest, and would have been best left undisturbed in its millennial rest.

Men no longer believed in such things, however. The old gods were forgotten, and the forests grew smaller and smaller. Industry demanded fuel for its fires and shipyards demanded wood for their hulls. Places that should have been left in sylvan silence forever now echoed with the ring of the axe.

There was blood on the axe.

Screaming woke him in the darkness. His heart thundered in his chest and his body trembled with shock and fever. How hot must he be to feel the mild, clammy air so cold against his skin? Such fever could destroy a man's brain. Nedelec had seen it happen to sailors before.

His vision was a blur of colours and shadows. Malevolent figures moved around him, not the clumsy staggering of invalid sailors, but the predatory grace of something stalking prey.

He swung his fists wildly and weakly, but connected only with empty darkness. His skin was burning and he realised that he could not trust his senses. Yet he felt it so strongly; a creeping malice was upon his ship, a presence that was inhuman and full of hatred.

The screaming stopped, and was replaced with a hoarse rasping moan, the sound of true horror. It turned Nedelec's stomach to cold water. Was every sailor dreaming the same dark dreams?

There was a whispering, as though the water that lapped against the hull spoke of a profound sorrow in a language that he could not understand. He forced himself to stand. His cabin spun. The walls were warped and the decking uneven. He staggered and closed his eyes, felt the deck slam against him as he fell, as hard and flat as ever.

'Can't trust my eyes,' he whispered to himself.

Feeling his way in the darkness he crawled from his cabin and onto the deck. He peered into the mist and darkness. He watched it distort before his eyes into trees that grew and twisted into a forbidding forest.

'Not real,' he muttered.

The creak and crack of wood drew his eyes as the figurehead reared and turned slowly towards him. The grim face twisted with contempt.

'It's a cursed ship isn't it, Captain?' Constant Pétibon crouched against the rail. 'Like the man said. We're a plague ship and we're cursed and we'll die out here. It's the devil, Captain, he's killing us. We have to swim for it.'

'You would drown, Constant. Look at you, you can't even stand!'

'I can't stay here with that thing. It keeps looking at me. It keeps whispering to me, Captain.'

Nedelec staggered over like a drunk and gripped the young man's shoulder.

'I can fix it, lad. You go back to your bunk. I have to get something.'

It took him a while to find, although the area below deck was quite small. It seemed to Captain Nedelec that he wandered through a forest of winding paths that stretched before him. As before, he closed his eyes and felt his way along the timbers of the hull, but he imagined now that he could feel rich dirt beneath his fingers and had to clamber over roots. He found the axe at last where he had known it would be. The handle was reassuringly solid and heavy in his grasp. He had once used this axe to hack through a broken mast on a schooner at the height of a storm. He knew its weight and balance like a fencer knew his sword.

A wild animal came at him from the shadows, screaming hoarsely as it scratched and bit him. He fought it, struck it away with weak hands until he could raise the axe above his head. The wild creature was Gordon, his first mate was mad with fever. The man was beyond reason. Captain Nedelec struck him with the blunt side of the axe head, once, twice, and Gordon fell still, moaning.

Nedelec panted with panic, then moved as fast as he could, dragging the axe behind him. Its weight scored the timbers as he made his way back above deck. He stumbled to his knees as he stepped into the mist.

The devil stood before him, tall and terrifying. The cold light of the moon framed the creature in silver. Its eyes were filled with sorrow and wrath as it looked down upon him.

'You humans and your axes,' its whisper was the sound of a growing storm within the leaves of trees. The devil's wooden flesh creaked as it moved towards him, 'You may wield destruction, but you cannot kill what cannot die.'

Nedelec gaped in horror as it stepped forward. Its cloven hooves grinding upon the deck as it leaned over him. Its antlers lowered like a stag as it breathed a creaking breath and spoke again.

'You are like mayflies with your brief lives. You cannot see the greater whole. You sow only seeds of death and you will reap your own destruction. But not soon enough. You tear the beating heart from the world. You choke her with the burning smoke of her own trees. You enslave and murder the wild creatures of her lands and consume the flesh of the dead like carrion eaters. You are a race of doom. You proliferate and spread like a festering corruption.

You have no respect.' The air hissed from wooden lungs as it drew near and its breath was the contagion that rotted the ship as it breathed and whispered, 'You must be torn away like dead wood in a storm. You must rot in the fallen leaves of time. You must die. You must *all* die.'

With every remaining ounce of strength, Captain Nedelec gripped the axe and swung upwards as he stood. He felt solid contact and hot moisture sprayed across his face. There was a single, shocked exhalation. With his eyes closed Nedelec flailed with the axe until his feet slipped in slick blood. He fell to his knees in exhaustion. A wave of dizziness took him and he sunk breathless, resting his face upon the festering wood of the deck as he fell unconscious.

He woke with the swell of the ocean as the deck lifted and fell beneath him. His eyes focused slowly on what lay before him.

There was blood on the axe.

There was blood on his hands.

There was blood on the deck and it pooled around the broken corpse that lay before him. The thin, pale body of Constant Pétibon was unnaturally twisted. His gaunt features were frozen in horror and spattered with blood. Nedelec stared without comprehension for a long moment before tears began to blur his vision with the realisation that he had killed the boy.

Intent returned slowly but insistently because it was all that Nedelec had left. The idea had taken root in his mind and now grew to fill all of his thoughts. Raising himself to his knees the Captain picked up the axe and wiped Pétibon's blood from the handle. He staggered to his feet and approached the figurehead, expecting it to turn and speak to him as it had the night before. Even as Nedelec began to swing the axe it remained motionless. The Captain was weak, and as each strike of the glistening axe head bit, only small chips of wood flew. His aim was poor, he was wheezing for breath and his arms ached, but he did not falter.

A slight breeze stirred, doing nothing to dispel the clinging fog, but cooling the sweat that drenched the Captain and making him shiver. The deck was rolling gently beneath his feet. The ship was no longer becalmed. He should try to rouse his crew perhaps and raise the sails, but not before his work here was done.

Again and again the axe fell, slowly deepening the cuts by tiny increments. Nedelec's fingers began to blister and bleed and his sickly arms trembled with the effort, but he did not relent.

With a crack like a whip, the wood under the axe began to separate. The weight of the figurehead itself was beginning to split the wood. The Captain found fresh energy. The deck began to heave and pitch beneath his feet, but Nedelec did not care. He had only a single purpose. His feverish mind had room for nothing else.

With popping sounds the figurehead began snapping away from the prow. The carving slowly, jerkily began to lean forward like a diver before twisting and slamming into the hull, then breaking away and plunging into the water, churning as it rolled face up and foundered.

The grim visage and reaching hands invited Nedelec to join it. Seaweed tangled in its antlers.

The Captain's hands were so stiff that he was almost unable to release the axe from his grip. He let it fall into the ocean where it was swallowed almost soundlessly by the rising waves.

With the last of his strength, tears running fresh down his cheeks, the Captain walked over and lifted the frail and broken corpse of Constant Pétibon into his arms. He dropped the young man's body over the rail into the arms of the ocean.

'I'm sorry, boy,' he whispered, 'I should have listened.'

Nedelec slid down onto the deck and closed his eyes, letting exhaustion swallow him. The rising storm lifted the waves until they began to flow across the deck, slowly washing away the blood that was congealing on the wood. Still the Captain did nothing. His crew were debilitated by sickness. The mist made it impossible to ascertain their bearings. It was not until the waves began to crash more forcefully across the deck, soaking him to the skin, that the Captain stirred and got to his feet. He ventured beneath the deck to lead his fevered and delirious crew, one by one, into the stormy night. They clung or tied themselves to the rigging for their own safety. Even if they had their bearings or were any of them able-bodied men, it would be impossible to sail against the fury of the ocean waves. Their only choice now was to ride out the storm without being washed overboard.

The rising wind began at last to tear away the clinging mist and, with a shock, Captain Nedelec realised that they were near land. His first instinct was one of pure joy. He would feel solid earth beneath his feet again. He would be rid of this foul ship and its curse. Then he saw the steep rise of the cliffs and the way the ocean hurled itself against them, and realised that they would be dashed against the rocks.

'Where is Pétibon?' Gordon called above the roaring ocean. The marks of the axe head were livid upon his temple.

'He tried to swim to shore,' Nedelec lied, 'to bring help.'

Gordon's expression was aghast and the Captain had to look away from him.

'This ship is evil,' Gordon's voice was little more than a whisper above the wind, 'it will be the death of us all.'

The grinding crunch of wood on rock jerked them all violently against the ropes that bound them to the rigging. One of the sailors began to weep, but the Captain could not see who it was. His own body shook as though palsied and he wondered if any of them had the strength to ride out the storm. The ship listed violently to one side as the tide dragged it off of the submerged rock, but the deck stayed listed to port and Gordon's grim shout of, 'The hull is breached. We're taking on water!' echoed his own horrified realisation.

'Abandon ship,' he whispered and then, louder, 'all hands abandon ship!'

Nedelec did not hesitate to join his men in unbinding themselves from the rigging and casting themselves into the cold sea. He had always believed that a Captain should go down with his ship, but he had no intention of being dragged down into darkness and death by this vessel. If he died, he intended to die free of its clinging curse.

They struck out as best they could with weak arms and shivering bodies. Gordon was the first to reach a rock high enough above the waves to serve as a temporary sanctuary. He helped haul the other sailors from the churning, roaring surf. They all pressed together, clinging for some semblance of warmth, as they watched *The Arden* listing closer to land before slamming into the cliffs. The ship broke apart against the jagged wall of stone, flung by a furious ocean and shattering into dark driftwood. The timbers ripped apart with a scream of tearing wood.

'Good riddance,' Captain Nedelec whispered and felt Gordon's strong fingers squeeze his arm in agreement.

Through the long night the storm howled and then fell as the tide receded. The surviving sailors huddled against the cold. At last, in the early morning of the next day, a shout from above on the cliffs told them that they had been discovered. The man who waved at them disappeared briefly, but then returned with long ropes to lower food and drink for them. Shortly after that other men appeared.

Having eaten and satisfied himself that his crew were safe, Captain Nedelec allowed himself to drift into unconsciousness. He did not wake again until he found himself wrapped in warm blankets. He soon discovered that he was in one of the rooms of the Priory Inn. The innkeeper was one of the men who had helped to rescue them from the sea.

The man, whose name was Jean Richardson, informed Aaron Nedelec gently that his ship had been destroyed and that the body of his lost man had washed up on the beach of Grève de Lecq.

'His name was Constant Pétibon,' Nedelec said sitting up and accepting a glass of water from Jean, 'he was a good man. The son of the owner. I don't know how I shall break this news to his father. The ship … it was completely destroyed?'

'I'm afraid so, Captain. Your cargo is lost as well. I am so sorry. The north of Jersey has a treacherous coastline.'

Nedelec nodded, hiding a look of relief that *La Josephine*, or *The Arden* as he had come to think of the ship, had been destroyed. *Cursed in the building. Cursed in the sailing.* Wasn't that what the superstitious Captain Teller had tried to warn him? Well she would be cursed in broken pieces on the floor of the ocean now, and he would never have to walk her deck again.

'One thing though,' Jean Richardson said with a half smile, 'the figurehead washed ashore in an open-topped cave called Le Creux de Vis. It's just a stone's throw from here. The locals call the place the Devil's Hole. There's damn fool people coming from all over to see the thing. They've even got a sculptor coming to give it legs and to prop it up like a statue. It's been putting money in my pockets all day what with all the people stopping in for a drink. The owner of the land says he's going to charge a fee to let people down to see it.'

Misreading Nedelec's expression, Jean Richardson faltered, 'Although I'm sure if you wished to take the thing back to the owner of *La Josephine*, when you return to France–'

'No!' Captain Nedelec's voice cracked with the force of his horror. 'Leave the damn thing where it is, or throw it back into the sea. I want nothing to do with it!'

Richardson smiled gently and patted his hand.

'I can see that you're still upset, Captain. As well you might be. I'll let you rest for now, but there's soup that will be ready in a little while and you should eat. Call out in the meantime if you need anything.'

A sickly feeling crept over Aaron Nedelec as he lay under blankets which no longer felt warm and, when he drifted into sleep, he dreamed. Dark dreams of an ancient forest where the wind whispered in the leaves.

ⵁ

They arrived in the night, the Prince Regent and the White Lady, meeting under the moonlight above Devil's Hole as though it had been prearranged.

'The wind spoke of his coming,' the Regent offered by way of explanation, 'the rain wept with his sorrow. Yet I did not think to see you here in the mortal world again.'

'I knew that *you* would come,' the White Lady said quietly as she looked down at the broken figurehead. 'His power dwarfs our own.

The trees sing of nothing else. They owe such fealty to him as they never will to me. He has woken something in the land.'

'Something wild,' the Regent agreed, 'I wish that he had come sooner, when his rage against the mortals might have benefited us.'

'I would prefer that he had not come at all, Regent,' the White Lady's voice, though soft as the breeze, held a note of annoyance. 'You still speak of an unwinnable war? Even after all this time? The age of the fae is over in this world.'

'Perhaps for now,' the Regent shrugged, 'yet we will endure. The mortals will destroy themselves sooner or later. Destruction is the abiding instinct of their kind. Would it really be so terrible to give them a little nudge towards their end?'

'Unleashing one of the old gods upon them would hardly be "*a little nudge*", Regent.'

The White Lady tucked a stray golden curl behind her ear before speaking again, 'His time was over even when our race was young. He must have slept for millennia upon millennia. It is a miracle that he woke at all.'

The Regent smiled and his white teeth glittered in the moonlight.

'You cannot kill what cannot die, my Lady. And of all of the lands in all of this vast world, the ocean brought him here. An *astonishing* coincidence.'

'I will not pretend to know the ways of the old gods, Regent,' the White Lady said looking away from his black gaze, 'I must presume he sensed something of the old magic, and that it drew him to us.'

'Perhaps. So what will you do with him now, my Lady? Kick him back into the ocean?'

The White Lady shot the Regent a withering glare and his handsome face lit up with laughter.

'I came to bring him home, as you have. He will have to be bound,' she said it softly as though expecting dissent, and her eyes searched his, 'we must do it before he regains his full strength.'

'Can you even bind such a thing, Aurora?' the Regent glanced down at the figurehead with a sceptical expression.

His use of her name caused her to startle slightly and she looked away before he noticed.

'I can try to bind him at least. With iron and with the stone keys. I may have time.'

The Regent sighed, 'Does your twisted tolerance for the mortals really stretch to risking your own existence?'

'It is a risk I must take,' the White Lady said firmly, 'he must be bound if he will not sleep. His rage consumes him and war with the mortals is certain death for all of our kind, Regent.'

'You are so sure of that, my Lady? They are so *weak*.'

'I have never been more certain of anything. They may be weak, but they are legion. Come, Regent, let us descend.'

He offered his arm, although they were both aware that she did not require his assistance. After a moment's hesitation, the White Lady rested her fingers lightly upon the black cloth of his jacket. With faultless grace, they made their way down the steep sides of Devil's Hole to the rocky inlet at its base. The last ripples of the receding tide whispered against the stones inside the narrow tunnel between the sea and the open cave. The figurehead lay upon its side like a corpse, yet the Regent could feel the power emanating from it so strongly that his steps faltered as he drew near. He saw the White Lady hesitate also, but then she took her hand from his arm and moved closer, kneeling at the devil's head. Aurora cradled the figurehead's cheek as one might comfort a sick child and said something softly, so softly that even the Regent's sharp ears could not make it out. Perhaps she spoke in the language of the trees, which was not his to understand. The words sounded like a benediction. Her delicate fingers traced the features of the wooden face, carefully, gently, and came to rest upon the devil's lips.

'You were sleeping when they came,' she said sadly, 'when they came with axes and took your home from you. We have come here tonight, we the leaders of both the Light and of the Dark, of the Seelie and the Unseelie Fae, together. We offer you a new home with us. Will you join us there in peace, old one? Will you share this last haven?'

As the Prince Regent watched, the wooden lips of the figurehead slowly parted and the White Lady of the Fae took something from its mouth. A large acorn rested within her hand and she held it up so that the Regent could see how it glowed before she secreted it within the folds of her gown.

'It seems you have your answer,' the Regent said with a small smile.

They made their way back up from the open cave and strolled together in a strangely comfortable silence until they reached the closest of the old stones at La Hougue des Géonnais, where they passed together into the realm of the fae.

And so the Devil of the Arden found a new home on the island of Jersey, seeping into its roots, spreading into its earth, and his rage did not diminish.

THE CROOKED FAIRY

The other children didn't like him.

The boy would have known that without being told, but the children told him anyway and they told him often.

'My mother says you're a changeling, Amory,' Jacque said to him loudly enough for the other children to hear how brave he was being.

'She says that sometimes the fairies come in the night and replace human babies with their own. She says that you were born with blue eyes like all redheads have. Then you got sick and you used to cry all the time, and everyone knew you were going to die. Then one morning when your mother checked on you, your eyes were *black* like they are now, and you weren't sick and you didn't cry anymore, not *ever*, and now you're just *weird*, Amory Harker.'

'All babies are born with blue eyes, Jacque,' the boy replied calmly, 'or that's what my own mother tells me at least.'

'She's not your real mother! *And* dogs are scared of you,' Jacque said, 'they're scared of you because you're a changeling and they can tell you're not normal.'

'Which dogs?' the boy asked, cocking his head curiously.

'*All* dogs,' Jacque said firmly. 'My mum says so. Everyone can tell you're not right and nobody wants you here.'

'Your mother seems remarkably well informed for someone who has never met me,' the boy remarked, tucking a red curl behind his ear, 'I am obliged to come to school to receive an education, Jacque, however you might happen to feel about it.'

He tried to smile, showing his crooked white teeth, and added, 'I suppose we'll just have to try to get along, Jacque. Perhaps we could even be friends?'

'I'll never be friends with you!' Jacque shouted, 'You're a changeling, Amory!'

'Do you know what a changeling is?' the boy asked.

Jacque hesitated, and then his face distorted and became pink, 'I *hate* you. We all hate you, Amory Harker!'

Jacque stormed away. His friends followed with a few backwards glances. The boy watched them go with a little frown.

One of the girls called back in a voice that quavered slightly, 'I hate you too, Amory Harker.'

'That's not my name,' the boy whispered quietly when they were out of earshot.

☙❧

Excluded from their company, he would sometimes follow the other children when they went to play after school had finished. He made sure to stay out of sight since the day that Liam Le Tiec had thrown a stone at him. If Amory did not want to be seen, they would not see him. It was as simple as that. He had learned to be secretive from a very young age, and there were things he knew to keep even from his mother. He never told her about the thrown stone. He suspected that the incident would have upset her a great deal more than it had upset him.

'You're a good boy, aren't you, Amory?' his mother would ask him.

Sometimes the question was purely rhetorical and she would ruffle his red crop of curls and hug him tight. On other days, the question seemed more a need for reassurance.

'I try my best to be a good boy, mother,' he would answer, and sometimes he would even remember to smile.

'Of course you do, Amory,' she would say then, and she would kiss his forehead and tell him that she loved him.

The boy loved her too. He did everything that he could to help her around the house, often astonishing her with the speed and efficiency with which he could complete tasks. Their vegetable garden thrived under his attention and their little crops were better than any that his mother could buy from the local farmers.

'He's just the best son I could hope for,' his mother had told their neighbour once in the boy's hearing, 'Amory's so clever! He never makes mistakes in his schoolwork. He solves mathematical problems that I can't even begin to understand myself, and I swear there's never a thing out of place in his room. He does nothing but read *and* he was walking before he was even one year of age.'

The neighbour had shot the boy a strange glance then, and Amory could tell that his mother regretted saying so much when she smoothed her skirt and said, tight-lipped, 'Not so unusual I suppose, for such a clever boy. Come on, Amory. Let's go back inside, my darling.'

'That's not my name,' he had whispered when he knew she could not hear him.

⁂

Perhaps he should have gone directly home after school each night because he knew his mother worried about him, yet he found the other children fascinating. He often followed them just to watch their strange games and listen to their odd disjointed conversations and outlandish boasts.

For the last few weeks, his quiet pursuit of them had led him most often to Fern Valley, where they would play around the shallow watercourse that meandered through the deep marshy grass. Cow parsley and stitchwort flowered white amidst the lush green. Dandelion seeds floated in the heavy air beneath the trees.

The children had learned a tale from one of the older girls, something that scared and excited them. They came here to dare each other to go alone along the footpath that circled the little valley. Up in the tree line they proved their bravery, running the narrow path, breathless with panic and laughter. They would go one at a time. Once each individual returned to the little group of friends, it was another child's turn to run the gauntlet.

The girls among the group would play a strange hand-clapping game where they faced each other in pairs and sang patty-cake rhymes as they slapped each other's palms. Their current favourite was the one that they had learned from the older girl who had informed them of the legend of Fern Valley.

From his position high up in the trees, the boy could hear the words as he watched Jacque sprint along the path and pass underneath his own hiding place.

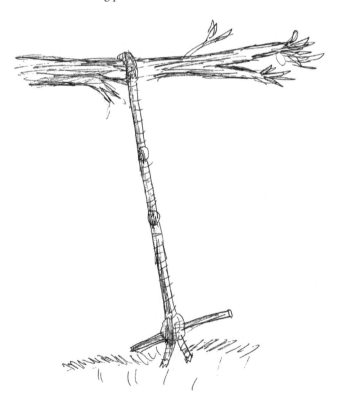

'*One, two, three, the crooked fairy,*' the girls sang, slapping their right hands up and their left hands down, then striking their knees and clapping.

The boy wrinkled his nose as he tried to follow the repetitive pattern of their hands, which accelerated as the rhyme continued. He would have liked to learn it so that he could play too, but he knew there would be no point in asking them to let him join in.

'*Four, five, six, he's made out of sticks.*'

Jacque was the second fastest runner in the group of children. There were seven of them here today, not counting himself. Two sets of girls playing patty-cake and three boys who always made a point of running first.

'*Sev-en, eight, don't be home late.*'

Amory couldn't help but feel that the girls had an unfair disadvantage, hampered as they were by their long skirts and the weight of their clothing. The boys could run along more freely in their short trousers and boots, without fear of their clothing or hair being caught in the brambles and the branches that lined the ill-tended path.

'*Nine and ten, he's going to kill again.*'

Little Nola Cauvain had caught her best dress on a blackthorn tree a week ago and torn a large chunk of the hem away. Her mother, the boy had overheard, had given her a slap for being so careless, but she'd run around the valley again the next night just the same.

'*Eleven, twelve, thirteen, he moves too fast to be seen.*'

Jacque arrived back at the starting point, red-faced and breathless but triumphant. Liam set off at once. Amory watched him sprint away; smiling slightly at the idea that Liam might trip over something and hurt himself.

As the girls accelerated to the end of the chant they speeded up to the point where they began to miss each other's hands and laugh hysterically, '*Fourteen, fifteen, sixteen, he'll eat your bones 'cause he's mean. Seventeen, eighteen, nineteen, twenty! The crooked fairy will leave you empty!*'

Almost as soon as they finished laughing, they started over again. '*One, two, three, the crooked fairy …*'

Once each child had run the path of an evening they would take turns playing on the swing which they had rigged from a thick branch with some old rope, swinging out over the shallow stream and back again. The boys tried to go as high as they could and the girls shrieked with excitement. Amory, who had tried the swing one evening when they had departed, could not see the appeal at all. Very little of what the children did made any sense to him. Especially that they appeared to want to risk their lives running around a valley which they had been told was the home of a particularly vicious monster. Either they believed in the creature, and should therefore stay away, or they did not believe in him and there was no point to their little ritual. Perhaps, Amory thought, he would never understand them. The thought made him a little sad.

Liam arrived back at the start, breathless and, to Amory at least, disappointingly unscathed.

'My turn!'

Rebecca, tall and dark-haired, broke away from the hand-slapping game and ran off without any further ceremony. Despite her long skirts, the boy judged her the fastest runner of the group. He liked Rebecca. She was never horrible to him and occasionally when their eyes met, she would compress her lips in something that almost resembled a smile. He sensed that she was embarrassed by the way her friends spoke to him.

'Play with me, Jacque?' Nola asked sweetly as Rebecca left her without a patty-cake partner.

Jacque, with a sigh that suggested the whole thing was utterly beneath him, took up the rhyme where Rebecca had broken off, *'Sev-en, eight, don't be home late, nine and ten, he's going to kill again, eleven, twelve, thirteen, he moves too fast to be seen—'*

Amory moved his lips in time to the rhyme. His black gaze followed Rebecca's progress along the path as she moved in and out of view between the trees. He heard her give a little shriek as she slipped in some mud, but she managed to keep her footing. The other children did not appear to hear. The boy had realised at a very young age that both his eyesight and his hearing were far more acute than those of the other children at his school. The fact that he could always hear them when they talked about him was just one of many things that he chose to keep to himself.

Rebecca was halfway around when the boy saw another figure moving through the trees. It was very fast, almost too fast to be seen, but the boy had different eyes than most and he saw it very clearly.

The crooked fairy descended from the trees like a spider, moving with the swift erratic motions of an insect. It froze to assess its surroundings with strange little twitches of its head. It held its long, clawed hands in front of itself with arms that seemed too long for its body. Its elbows were hunched low in front of it. The crooked fairy reminded the boy of a picture he had seen in a library book of a creature called the praying mantis.

The boy could see sharp fangs in a face dominated by jaws, high cheekbones and large eyes as white as the boy's own were black.

When the crooked fairy began to run through the trees, it used its long arms in addition to its legs, propelling itself with breathtaking speed on all fours. On its back were tiny, useless vestigial wings. It was unclothed except for a chain around its neck, which held a small pendant.

If it chose to pursue Rebecca, it could certainly catch her before she reached the other children. Not that getting back to their company could possibly offer her any protection from such a creature.

Amory watched in horror as the crooked fairy moved in a burst of speed from one tree trunk to the next and peered slowly around at the children playing at the far end of the little valley. It froze again, motionless except for the strange chattering grind of its sharp teeth. The creature sniffed the air then, and saliva began to trickle from between its jaws and down its chin.

The boy could see Rebecca in his peripheral vision moving back towards the other children on her swift feet, but he dared not take his black gaze from the crooked fairy for fear of losing sight of the creature.

In another burst of speed, the crooked fairy moved to the path and dipped its head down to the ground to sniff where the children had passed by. It tilted its head to the side and then, stepping back slowly off the path, it hunched down like a crab in the long grass and cow parsley, and settled motionless to wait.

If the boy had not seen it hide there, he would never have noticed it.

Rebecca arrived back with the other children and dropped a dramatic curtsy as Jacque applauded her speed.

'You now, Nola,' she laughed.

Amory began to move swiftly. He leapt from his own tree into the one next to it, and then dropped quickly through the branches down onto the path, out of sight of the children and ahead of Nola. He moved behind a tree as she began her circuit of the little valley and he could hear her pounding footsteps approaching.

As she passed, Amory lunged out and pulled Nola into the bushes, so fast that she didn't even have time to scream. His hand was over her mouth. She struggled wildly, but the boy was very strong.

'Be quiet, Nola,' he said softly, 'it's here. It's come. Look there, between the trees, underneath the lilac flowers.'

Still holding his hand over her mouth, he pointed ahead. He could see Nola's gaze flick wildly, missing the crooked fairy, and then he felt her inhale sharply.

'Do you see it?'

She nodded as the colour drained from her face, her wide blue eyes turned to his as she looked back at him in horror.

'Go to the others,' he told her, 'do it now. Tell them to run.'

Nola didn't argue but fled back the way she had come immediately when he released her.

He heard her little voice high with panic moments later, 'Rebecca! Jacque it's *here*. We have to go. We have to go *now*!'

The sound of children's laughter greeted her words, and the boy sighed.

Of course. Of course they would not believe her until they had seen the crooked fairy with their own eyes, and by then it would be too late.

'Amory showed me, I *saw* it!' Nola was saying, her voice near tears, 'Let's go, *please*!'

'Amory Harker is *here*?' the boy heard Liam Le Tiec exclaim. 'Who does he think he is following us, the little creep?'

'Oh for goodness sake, Liam!' Rebecca said, 'What difference does it make? You don't *own* this valley you know.'

'We have to *go*!' Nola was almost hysterical.

Shooting a glance back, Amory could see her hauling uselessly on Jacque's arm.

'We have to go now!'

'Don't be so stupid, Nola,' Jacque exclaimed, shaking her off, 'there's no such thing as the crooked fairy. Harker's just trying to scare you.'

The crooked fairy shifted impatiently, shedding leaves as it came out of the undergrowth, like a trapdoor spider emerging from its lair. It sniffed the air again. Its dead white eyes narrowed and its head twitched in the direction of the children. Dropping forward on its long arms, it began to move towards the sound of their voices.

'Show me where Harker is,' Jacque demanded of Nola.

Amory wondered if he would die here, trying to protect these children who did not even like him.

'Where are you, changeling?' Liam shouted.

Amory winced. Sometimes they would chant that word, over and over again, out of earshot of the teachers, '*Changeling, changeling, changeling.*'

Usually he would stand impassively, with his head tilted to the side and meet their eyes with his black gaze until they grew uncomfortable and their chanting stopped. Today he would not have time to be so patient.

He stepped out from the shadows and the concealment of the trees and began to walk down the bank into the low open valley towards the stream. The long grass and reeds brushed his legs, whispering with each step as he placed himself in the path of the crooked fairy.

'There he is, the little creep!' Liam exclaimed as he spotted Amory.

The red-haired boy ignored him, his eyes fixed on the tree line.

'Hey, *changeling*!' Jacques shouted. 'What are you doing here, changeling?'

The crooked fairy emerged into the light, blinking its white eyes. It shook its head in the sunlight, spraying saliva. Its gaze lit upon Amory and its wide mouth gaped wider, revealing a row of grinning white teeth each as long as Amory's fingers. Hunched as the creature was, it was difficult to assess its true size. Amory suspected that, had it stood straight on its spidery legs and unfolded its crooked spine, it would have been at least twice his height. In the daylight, its dappled skin was the greenish grey of necrotic flesh.

Amory squared his narrow shoulders and stood his ground as the crooked fairy began to move towards him, knuckling forward swiftly.

Nola's scream cut through the valley, silencing the shouting of the boys and causing the crooked fairy to pause, raising its clawed hands as though to test the air, like a spider feeling vibrations on its web.

'Run!' Amory shouted over his shoulder, but the children were frozen with disbelief and terror. He turned then, and in the voice of something that was not a child he roared at them, *'Run!'*

The children finally began to move. Nola was sobbing with horror. Amory hoped that they would not look back. As he turned to face the crooked fairy, it leaped forward with astonishing speed.

There was nothing Amory could do to evade it.

He was slammed into the mud by the force of the attack and he cried out as the crooked fairy's long claws stabbed through his chest like sabres, smashing through his rib cage and pinning him to the ground. The crooked fairy grinned. Saliva dripped from its massive jaws, splattering Amory's throat. A stone pendant around its neck spun and swung in front of the boy's face.

Then the crooked fairy's gaze lifted and followed the direction in which the other children were running. Its pupils widened like a cat on the hunt. It withdrew its talons from Amory's chest. They were red with the boy's blood.

Amory struggled to inhale as the crooked fairy stood and moved off after the other children with its sharp erratic movements. The monster was almost to the path when Amory called after it.

'Excuse me!' he shouted hoarsely, standing and brushing mud from his trousers.

The crooked fairy halted and spun in surprise, slamming its claws down into the mud and turning its head violently to the side in confusion.

Amory looked down at his chest. The deep, penetrating wounds closed and healed without the hint of a scar, and with a shrug of his shoulders, Amory snapped his ribs back into place and inhaled deeply into his healing lungs.

The crooked fairy chattered and ground its teeth curiously.

'I'm afraid you'll have to do better than that,' Amory said, straightening his shredded shirt as best he could and raising up lightly on his toes in preparation.

'Well, well, well, what do we have here?' the crooked fairy rasped.

Amory took a step back, so startled was he to hear the creature speak.

'Cat got your tongue?' it hissed, and then it came towards him wielding its clawed hands like blades, slashing and thrusting, a blur of motion.

Amory whirled away. Even though he was prepared for its speed, he was barely able to stay out of its reach.

He ducked and dodged as the fairy's filthy talons whipped past him, using all of his own unnatural agility to stay out of reach, barely, just barely, as the fairy hissed in annoyance.

'Not a real boy, are you, little one?' the crooked fairy snarled, 'Something else, something *different*.'

'Depends on how you look at it,' Amory gasped, stumbling back from a vicious slash that drew a line of red across his cheek.

'How will you taste, I wonder? What sort of delicious treat will you be?'

The crooked fairy paused and licked Amory's blood from the tip of its claws, 'Ah … I know that flavour, little *cuckoo*. Do your little friends know what you are?'

'They're not my friends.'

Amory turned and broke for the trees, sprinting away from the exit to the valley, leading the crooked fairy away from the children. A line of fire cut across his back as the fairy caught up to him and he gasped with pain as he threw himself up the bank. The cut was already healing as he turned and leant backwards with supernatural speed to avoid a slash of claws that would have slit his throat.

'Fast aren't you, little cuckoo?' The crooked fairy seemed almost pleased with the challenge that Amory presented, 'Not fast enough though, I think. And young, oh so *very* young.'

'Yes, and small,' Amory remarked as he jumped into the lowest branches of the trees.

The crooked fairy snarled and came after him, its long limbs thrashing against branches. It was slowed by its size, even as its strength snapped twigs and tore through leaves that Amory had to dodge around. It bent the smaller trees with its weight as it pursued him.

'So you have to run and hide do you, little cuckoo? Too young to have all your powers then? Too young to fly away little cuckoo, and far too young to be wise!'

Amory concentrated on staying ahead of the creature, using his smaller size and agility to move up into the thinner branches where the crooked fairy's weight caused the trees to stir beneath it. The fairy slowed as it had to allow for the sway of branches, but to Amory the sound of grinding teeth seemed no further behind.

The boy's mind raced desperately as he scrabbled and leapt from tree to tree, weaving between the narrow trunks, swinging from branches and running along boughs as nimble as a squirrel. It was only a matter of time before he made a mistake, missed a step, or slowed for long enough that the crooked fairy would be upon him. He knew that the next time the monster had him in its claws, there would be no more chances. He risked a glance backwards and saw the crooked fairy's pale eyes fixed upon him. The slit pupils were wide in the deathly pale of its eyes. It used its claws to tear twigs and leaves out of its path, cutting a swathe through the foliage in its determined pursuit.

Amory needed something: a weapon or a plan, or even a line of escape that would not lead the creature back towards the children. He willed Rebecca and her friends to move faster, to run and keep running until they reached their homes. He wondered if his body would be found hollowed out the way the children's rhyme described.

Amory knew he could not fight the crooked fairy. The creature was correct in its assumption that he was young and that his powers were limited. He gritted his teeth in annoyance. Maybe if he had spent less time trying to fit in and be like the children around him, and more time learning to be what he really was, he would have had a greater chance of surviving. Such regrets would not serve him now however.

His black eyes flashed around him and something caught his eye.

With only the slightest notion of a plan, Amory changed direction sharply, dropping to catch a branch with his fingertips and swing almost directly under the crooked fairy, who let out a snarl and dropped with a crashing of branches to follow him. It launched itself from a tree trunk and Amory cried out as talons cut across his back. The force of the attack threw him forwards and he only just managed to get a hand on a branch and swing onwards and out of reach. He ran swiftly along a bough and dived, lower, landing on his hands and running on all fours before leaping for the branch that he needed.

He grabbed at the rope of the children's swing, where it was knotted around the branch, and then began to haul on it. There was no time, but panic made him swift as he dragged the rope up into his arms.

The crooked fairy landed with an impact that shook the thick branch and made it bend. Amory began to back away towards the narrow end of the bough, out over the valley and the narrow stream. The crooked fairy grinned and chattered its teeth.

'What do you think you're doing now, little cuckoo?'

It moved forward slowly and the branch began to lower beneath its weight. Amory wondered whether it would snap and send them both tumbling to the muddy ground. He wondered who would get up first. He suspected it would not be him.

'Do you think I'm going to stand still, little cuckoo, while you tie me up?'

'Well if you would be willing, that would certainly help me,' Amory said as calmly as he could manage.

He gripped the rope in one hand. It was thicker than his thumb. Fisherman's hemp rope, durable and strong, probably supplied by Rebecca's father who ran a fishing boat out of St Helier harbour.

'Or were you planning to try and kill me with that twig?' The crooked fairy tilted its head at an almost impossible angle and drool dripped from its mouth.

Amory hefted the small branch of the swing in his other hand and shrugged.

'I'm certainly planning to try. Come closer. Let's see what happens.'

'I'll still catch them, you know,' the crooked fairy hissed, inching closer.

'No you won't,' Amory said quietly, but he wondered if he said it more to reassure himself.

He bounced up and down a little on the flexible branch, like a diver on a board, and with an annoyed chatter of teeth the crooked fairy placed its claws down to help keep its balance.

Amory dived, not down, but back towards the crooked fairy. He was fast, but claws still raked him as he slid through the crooked fairy's legs. He stopped as swiftly as he had leapt. The crooked fairy struggled to turn its strange body to face him and Amory flung the gathered rope and wooden swing around and through its legs, once, then twice. As talons slammed into his back like sword blades, he grasped the rope to his chest and let himself drop like a stone.

With a grinding shriek, the crooked fairy was pulled down by its own claws where they were anchored in the changeling's back. It fell awkwardly, only to find its long legs tangled in the rope. It was jerked to a sudden halt, where it swung and flailed.

Amory, ignoring the white-hot pain of the crooked fairy's claws tearing from his back, climbed up the rope and over the creature's back onto the branch. His blood dripped down and onto the fairy's face as it snarled at him. It slashed wildly at his legs and arms as Amory backed away, wrapping the rope repeatedly around the branch and knotting it as best he could.

'You think *this* will hold me, little cuckoo?'

'Not for long,' Amory allowed, 'long enough though, I imagine.'

The crooked fairy began to hack angrily at the rope with its filthy claws. The hemp began to fray, but held firm.

With a little hop Amory dropped from the branch and down into the valley below. As he hit the ground one of his ankles broke with a sharp crack. He took a moment and a deep breath as it fixed. Then with a few shaky steps to test it, Amory broke into a run.

'I will find you, little cuckoo!' the crooked fairy called. 'I will sniff you out and hunt you down when you come back to us, changeling boy!'

Amory cast a glance back over his shoulder.

'You look *very* foolish!' he called and then shouted with surprise as Rebecca stepped into his path, her skin white with dread and her eyes tear-filled.

'Why are you still here?' Amory demanded, grabbing her arm and hauling her with him more roughly than he had intended, 'I told you to run! Did I not tell you to run?'

'I couldn't just leave you!' Rebecca exclaimed grabbing the hem of her skirts and trying to match his pace, 'You could have been killed!'

'And if I had been killed, *you* would have been next. What value would there have been in both of us dying? Really there is no logic in your reasoning, Rebecca.'

'I couldn't just leave you,' she repeated, 'you saved us!'

Amory took her hand to pull her faster as they left the valley and made for town down the hill.

'Perhaps I did save you, but it was far more likely that I would fail in the attempt.'

'So where was *your* logic in trying?' Rebecca demanded breathlessly.

'I don't know. I was just trying to slow him down. Please stop talking and run, your lungs are small and weak and require as much air as they can get. If the crooked fairy gets free I won't be able to stop it again.'

He did not let her rest or falter, and by the time they reached her home, Rebecca was wheezing and red-faced with her dark hair in disarray.

She waved him off as he tried to lead her up to her front door, and sat down upon the wall of the garden to get her breath.

'He can't catch us now,' she coughed and stared up at Amory standing before her. Amory was not at all out of breath and this fact did not escape the little girl.

'I'm afraid I may have broken your swing,' Amory said apologetically, 'but it's not safe to go back to Fern Valley again, so I suppose that it doesn't really matter …'

'I saw what you did,' Rebecca said, but her tone was not accusatory, 'I saw him hurt you, and you just got up. I saw the way you moved, Amory, and how fast you were. Nobody can move like that. You *are* a changeling, aren't you? It's all right. I won't tell.'

Uncertain how to respond, Amory just regarded her with his large black eyes.

'I mean, you're a changeling, but you're not *bad*, are you? You can't be bad, or you wouldn't have saved us,' she smiled. 'We could be friends if you like?'

'Thank you,' the boy said, and then he remembered to return her smile.

Rebecca gave a shaky laugh, 'You really need to practise the way you use your face, Amory. Oh dear … look at the state of you.'

Her vague gesture encompassed his torn clothing and the blood that had soaked him in his battle with the crooked fairy.

'Does your mother know? About you, I mean,' Rebecca enquired.

'I don't believe she wants to know,' Amory said carefully, 'she has never asked.'

Rebecca nodded thoughtfully.

'Well, I think perhaps you should tell her that you fell off of the swing into some thorns and had a nosebleed. That should explain the blood and tearing at least. Although not why you have no scratches I suppose …'

Amory looked down at his hands and frowned; then he closed his eyes to concentrate. Rebecca gasped in astonishment as tiny scratches formed and crawled across the boy's skin. He looked down at his hands speculatively.

'That'll do,' Rebecca said with a shaky laugh, 'should I come home with you and vouch for you?'

'No, you stay here where it's safe. Can we really be friends?' the boy asked quickly, 'You're not afraid?'

'No, of course not!' Rebecca jumped up and gave him a quick hug, 'I should go and clean up before my father gets home. I'll see you at school tomorrow, and you can tell me what else you can do, Amory Harker!'

The boy watched her go inside with his black eyes. Then he whispered, quietly, and with a little smile, 'That's not my name.'

GOBLIN GOLD

'It's a big rock,' Madelaine said dubiously.

'Yes,' Hubert said, 'it's a menhir. Legend has it that sometimes, at midnight on a full moon—'

'It's just,' Madelaine held up her hands to stop his explanation and then spread her palms with a smile, 'Hu, your history with big rocks isn't very encouraging.'

Hubert laughed and gathered his wife in his arms, planting a firm kiss on her forehead.

'No witches this time, I promise you, Madelaine. Just a lovely evening away from home, and maybe a *tiny* adventure.'

'Well, I brought my spoon just to be on the safe side.'

Madelaine patted the pocket of her old blue dress and then tilted her head to rest it on Hubert's chest as she looked at the menhir more closely.

It was a large standing stone of grey and pink granite, a little taller than Hubert. It was wide at the base and rose to a point, jutting up like a stalagmite. Its surface was dappled with patches of yellow lichen and veined with quartz crystal. It stood alone in the otherwise barren landscape.

All around them sand dunes and sea-grass stretched along the great curve of St Ouen's Bay. This area was different to any other in Jersey, appearing more like a desert in contrast to the rich dark farmland and woods of the rest of the island. It was as though the ocean had reached in to bury this area of land with sand, salting the earth and destroying the fertile ground. Only tough grass, coarse heather and gorse thrived here. The small twisted trees that struggled to survive were bent low to the ground like little old men worn down by eroding winds from the sea.

It was strangely beautiful under the blue summer sky. Skylarks called as they hung on the air. Rabbits darted through the low patches of scrub, watching Madelaine and Hubert curiously. Huge breaking waves beat against the sandy shore in a relentless roar and retreat.

'Why do you have the shovel, Hu?' Madelaine asked him as he released her from his embrace. 'Please tell me it isn't my cooking. You didn't bring me out here to bang me on the head with it and bury me, did you?'

'Of course not. I would love you more than life, even if your cooking was *twice* as bad as it is, Madelaine,' Hubert said sweetly, and then dodged away from a playful slap before it could make contact.

Madelaine shook her head at him, trying not to laugh as she straightened her necklace of painted wooden beads.

'Well just for that, Hu, *you* can make dinner tonight. Shall we set up a camp now? It will be dark in a few hours and I'm exhausted. We've walked across the whole island! How many miles do you think? Ten?'

'At least ten I'd say. My feet feel more like it was fifty. I might go and dip them in the sea. I think I have a blister coming.'

'You go and paddle. I'll find a place to set up and start looking for some wood and sticks to build a fire. We probably should have gathered some as we walked, it's so barren here.'

'I'll find some when I get back. You just have a rest, love.'

Hubert kissed her on the cheek and left his pack leant against the menhir as he walked towards the sea. Madelaine watched him go with a smile.

She wandered a little further inland away from the standing stone and put her things near the slope of a grassy dune. She laid out some blankets to sit on, pulled her shoes and socks off, and buried her toes in the sand. Smiling, she looked over at the menhir thoughtfully, enjoying the sun on her face. The large stone certainly didn't look dangerous, just unusual, jutting up incongruously from such a featureless landscape. Laying down on the blankets, she closed her eyes and gave a sigh of satisfaction. She realised that she'd interrupted Hubert before he could explain the legend that had brought them here. Something about the menhir and a full moon …

She awoke to cool darkness, hours later, uncertain for a few moments where she was. Her hand crept out across the blanket, seeking Hubert, but he was not beside her. Above, hanging in the sky was the full moon, startlingly bright in a starry night. Madelaine shivered and propped herself up on one elbow with a yawn.

A small fire lit up the menhir stone. Hubert must have built it while she was sleeping. The flickering light leapt and fell, throwing erratic shadows behind it, and she rubbed her eyes vigorously to clear her blurred vision. The fire was set between where she lay and the menhir, making it harder for her to see. The movement of the light gave the strange impression that Hubert was dancing.

Madelaine watched sleepily for a few moments and then sat up frowning.

Hubert *was* dancing. Like a wild man, he jumped and spun, with none of the careful grace or dignity he had exhibited during their wedding waltz. He looked frenzied, almost demented. Madelaine gave a snort of laughter and was about to call out to him when she noticed smaller shapes moving in the light and inhaled sharply, her fingers flying to her lips in shock. What she had at first mistaken for small shadows cast by Hubert and the movement of the flames were actually little figures, no taller that Hubert's waist. They too were dancing, in and out of the firelight, around and around the standing stone.

Above the crackling of the flames, Madelaine could make out a low hum, like a wordless song, and as she heard it, she stumbled to her feet. She exclaimed at the involuntary movement, and then yelped as she found herself skipping towards them. It was as though some puppet master had control of her legs and arms. She screamed as she almost danced directly into the fire, but at the last moment her feet began to move her counter-clockwise around the menhir and she was lost in the dance. She fought to control her body as she whirled and spun, her feet dancing an energetic jig that she barely knew.

'Oh no, Madelaine!' Hubert gasped.

His face was red with exertion and sweat beaded his forehead, but Madelaine had barely glanced at him before her gaze lit upon one of the little dancing figures and she gave a shout of surprise.

The creature was dancing with glee, its ugly face split into a huge grin full of little sharp teeth as it waved bony arms and legs. It had large pointed ears, and greenish skin that looked a sickly yellow in the firelight. A simple loincloth was tied under its little round belly and it cackled and jumped as Madelaine looked at it.

'Another for the dance!' it croaked and capered wildly before continuing its low humming song.

The other little monster looked very similar, only it was taller, painfully thin and had long, stringy hair. It danced with just as much enthusiasm and its nasal song did not falter as it fastened its beady eyes on her and flailed its limbs.

'Hubert!' Madelaine shouted, meeting his eyes briefly before her own spinning dance turned her away from him.

'I'm sorry, Madelaine,' Hubert gasped, 'I didn't think … I didn't know that this would happen.'

In the light of the fire, Madelaine could see that the silver charm that Hubert wore on his necklace had fallen outside of his shirt, and no part of it was touching his skin.

'Well what was supposed to happen?' Madelaine asked as she danced into a small hole at the base of the menhir and fell over Hubert's shovel, stubbing her toe.

For a second she lay flat on her stomach, but then her feet fought her to a standing position and she was dancing again. She bared her teeth in a hiss of discomfort as each dancing step shot a lance of pain through her injured foot.

'Are you alright?' Hubert demanded.

'No, I'm not alright!' Madelaine said indignantly. 'My toe hurts and I'm dancing around a big stone in the dark with … with … oh what are these *ghastly* little people?'

'Goblins I think?'

'*Goblins!*' the first of the creatures confirmed, nodding enthusiastically before resuming his low hum.

'Why are we dancing, Hubert? I can't control my body. This is horrible!'

'I don't know, it's some sort of magic. Where's your spoon, Madelaine?'

'It's in my, *ouch*! I trod on a stone. It's in my pocket, Hubert, but I can't control my stupid hands.'

'The more you fight it, the worse it gets. Just relax and it's not so tiring.'

Madelaine spun like a ballerina, her arms lifted above her head and she found herself leaping, not at all of her own volition.

'How long have you been dancing, Hu?'

'About an hour I think,' Hubert admitted miserably, 'I definitely do have a blister now.'

'Well good, you deserve it!' Madelaine exclaimed. 'Oh, why didn't you wake me up?'

'I wanted to surprise you,' Hubert said miserably.

'With *goblins*?'

'No, Madelaine, with treasure.'

'Thieves! Disgusting thieves! Come to steal our treasures!' the fat goblin shouted, waving its little fists at Hubert without ceasing its dance.

'How dare you?' Madelaine snapped at it, then tried to compose herself as her legs spun her into a graceful cotillion step and then began to waltz, her arms holding an invisible partner. The weight of the silver spoon in her pocket tapped gently against her leg as she swayed.

'You stop this,' Madelaine shouted at the fat goblin, 'you stop it at once, do you hear?'

The goblin cackled and then continued to sing.

'Hubert, *what* treasure? I know you're out of breath, but please try to explain.'

'You're so graceful, Madelaine,' Hubert said.

'For goodness *sake*, Hu!'

'Sorry. There's a legend that if you dig under the fairy stones on a full moon sometimes you find treasure,' Hubert paused to try and catch his breath, and then went on, 'I thought that this one, being so remote out here, might never have been tried. And you said you'd never seen this part of the island so …'

'Thief!' squawked the goblin.

'Be quiet, you little monster,' Madelaine said, then asked. 'Where did the goblins come from?'

'I don't know. One moment I was digging, then my shovel hit something and the next minute I was dancing around like an idiot.'

'Well what do we do?'

'There are … there are legends of people dancing themselves to death, Madelaine. That's why I didn't call out to you. I thought it would be better …'

'To break my heart when I found you dead in the morning instead? Oh I would box your ears if I had any control over my limbs, Hubert Vautier.'

'Dance to death, dance to death, and when you die we'll take that treasure off your neck!' The goblin shrieked in delight, eyeing the coloured wooden beads Madelaine wore at her throat.

In the firelight the goblin's eyes burned red.

'So help me, when I stop dancing I am going to beat you to death with that shovel,' Madelaine told the little man.

The goblin gave a tiny scream and danced further away from Madelaine.

'The girl one is frightening!' it shouted to its companion, who danced closer to Hubert without ceasing its nasal hum.

'Kick them if you get a chance,' Madelaine said, 'I think if they stopped singing the spell would be broken.'

'You're horrible and I hate you!' the fat goblin said before swiftly disappearing out of sight behind the menhir.

'Yes, I am horrible,' Madelaine shouted, 'and when I catch you, I'm going to steal your treasure and throw it in the sea.'

'No, not the treasures!' the goblin slapped its own head in distress and danced an agitated jig.

Madelaine couldn't respond as her body performed a series of spirited pirouettes, lifting her graceful hands above her head and bruising her bare toes painfully upon the ground. An elegant swooping bow caused the spoon in her pocket to lift and drop, banging against her leg again. Madelaine frowned.

Hubert was correct. If she stopped fighting the strange control over her body, the dance had an economy of motion that was less tiring. With this in mind, Madelaine tried something different. She concentrated, and as each motion began she embraced it, attempting to fulfil each step and gesture with all the grace at her command. Despite her aching feet and breathless exhaustion, she danced with everything she had, revelling in the beauty of movement, finding a strange rhythm in the goblin's song. She spun and gestured, using every part of her body from her toes to her fingertips to embrace the magic. She jumped and twirled and she leapt like a ballerina until eventually, with a little thud, her silver spoon fell out of her pocket and landed on the sandy ground.

Madelaine gave a sob of relief.

Hubert saw the spoon as he danced past, and Madelaine saw his limbs twitch with the effort to reach for it.

'It's no good!' he exclaimed in frustration, but Madelaine did not try to bend down as she danced another circuit around the menhir. She simply placed her artful feet with care, and as her twirling steps led her back towards the spoon, she placed her bare foot upon it.

It was like stepping on a chunk of ice. The second her toes made contact with the silver, the marionette strings of magic snapped and Madelaine gasped as she dropped to her knees, groping under her bare foot with shaking fingers until the spoon was safely in her grasp.

Then like a pouncing cat, Madelaine jumped and grabbed the fat goblin by one of his scrawny arms. She bounced the bowl of the spoon off of his forehead as though she were smashing the top of an egg.

He yelped and wriggled.

'Where's the treasure?' she demanded.

'Ow, take the nasty silver away. It's *our* treasure, ours, all ours!'

'Don't be greedy,' Hubert gasped as he pirouetted past, 'we only want a little bit.'

'Let Greem *go*,' the skinnier goblin finally ceased his singing to protest in a reedy voice, 'don't kill Greem with the fearsome weapon!'

As the song ceased Hubert collapsed in a heap, wheezing on the sand.

'This weapon is lethal,' Madelaine said, brandishing the spoon at the thin goblin.

'Run, Blu, run, save yourself!' Greem wailed.

Hubert locked his grip around Blu's skinny leg before the little creature could flee. Then he pulled his silver charm necklace under his shirt and against his skin with his free hand.

'Nobody's going anywhere until I see some treasure,' Madelaine said firmly.

The fat goblin struggled in her grip, but Madelaine, panting and furious, her black hair wild from dancing, held him firm.

'*Thieves*,' Greem said petulantly stamping his little foot.

'I'll give you the treasure,' skinny Blu whispered, 'please don't kill my Greem.'

'I'm not going to *kill* him,' Madelaine said indignantly.

'She might,' Hubert said sharply, 'she's unpredictable. Always killing people, my wife is. You'd best get that treasure as fast as you can.'

Blu dived towards the menhir so quickly that Hubert let go of him in surprise. Throwing the shovel to one side the skinny goblin began to dig with his hands, sending up a shower of sand like an enthusiastic dog. He emerged with a small iron-bound chest the size of a cabbage.

Madelaine and Hubert exchanged excited glances and Greem began kicking angrily at the dirt.

'Well then,' Hubert said taking the chest and setting it on the ground, 'let's have a look, shall we?'

The hinges opened with a rusty creak and the lid fell back.

Madelaine gave a little gasp. Her grip upon the fat goblin relaxed and he pulled free, running to his companion's side where they embraced as though separated for weeks, and glared at the married couple.

'Why do they steal our treasure from us, Greem?' Blu asked pitifully.

'Nasty, awful humans,' Greem said darkly, 'they are *monsters*.'

Hubert stirred the contents of the chest with his strong fingers, sifting through ancient gold coins. He placed a blue shell and a piece of broken green glass in his palm and then held a broken ormer shell up to the goblins. The mother of pearl inside glittered in the firelight.

'Why are these in here?' he asked.

Greem covered his mouth with horror.

'See how he covets the precious treasures, Blu?' he whispered through his gnarled fingers. 'He wants all the *shiny* things, the horrid thief.'

'These?' Hubert tilted his head. 'These are worthless though.'

'Oh horrid humans, liars and thieves, we should have eaten them, Blu. They can never be trusted. See how that girl one has a king's ransom at her throat, yet still she wants more!'

Madelaine put her hand up to her necklace of painted wooden beads and raised an eyebrow.

Hubert frowned and dropped the shiny objects back into the little chest.

'All that glitters is not gold,' he said to Madelaine, holding up a little nugget of fool's gold that might be found washed up on the beach. He saw that she too realised the goblins were like magpies. They sought out and kept shiny objects. To them the fact that some were worth a fortune in the human world was incidental and unimportant. A pretty shell to them was worth as much as a ruby.

Hubert cleared his throat.

'I only meant that, compared to my wife's magic treasure necklace, these things are worth very little.'

'Treasure necklace?' Madelaine said, and then nodded quickly, 'Oh, well yes, it is very precious of course, because it ...' she glanced at Hubert desperately.

'Helps you find treasure,' Hubert finished calmly.

'I expect that *you* would like such a thing?' Madelaine asked the goblins haughtily, putting a hand on her hip.

'Such a rare treasure,' Greem whispered.

'Sometimes we wake up in the morning, and there's treasure, just scattered about all over the place,' Hubert added, 'we don't know what to do with it half the time.'

Blu closed his eyes in ecstasy at the thought.

'Frankly I'm sick of it,' Madelaine said. 'Treasure all over the place making a mess. And here we are again, with more treasure,' she gestured impatiently at the chest, 'and I myself am only really partial to gold.'

'And diamonds,' Hubert added swiftly, holding up a gemstone the size of a pea, 'why I expect you'd quite like to trade that annoying necklace, wouldn't you, Madelaine? If only *somebody* would want it.'

Blu's fingers twitched and Greem began whispering loudly in his companion's ear.

'Well I couldn't just give it away,' Madelaine said carefully, 'it does have some sentimental value, after all.'

'Obviously,' Hubert said solemnly.

'Ten gold coins and a diamond for the treasure necklace!' Greem shouted.

'Why, that would be daylight robbery!' Hubert protested.

'Fifteen coins and two diamonds!'

'I couldn't possibly accept less than three diamonds,' Madelaine said, 'did I mention it has sentimental value?'

'Fifteen gold and all the stupid boring diamonds?' Greem offered.

'Done!' Madelaine unclasped her painted wooden beads and tossed them to Blu, who caressed each bead like a precious rosary.

Hubert counted out the coins and pocketed four diamonds.

Madelaine sat down suddenly and gave a little laugh.

'Well,' said Hubert, his voice quavering a little, 'it's been a pleasure doing business with you gentlemen. I would shake your hands, but I'm worried you might bite my fingers off.'

He slowly handed the little treasure chest to Greem. The little goblin wrapped his arms around it protectively and sniffed it.

Blu had reverentially fastened Madelaine's necklace around his scrawny throat and bared his fangs in a delighted grin.

'Let's go home now,' Greem said, tucking the treasure chest under one arm and reaching out to clasp Blu's hand, 'I don't like these big monsters, they're rude.'

Blu gave a short, sharp nod and reached into his loincloth, producing a little flat stone with the symbol of an anchor on it.

'What's that?' Hubert asked, but even as the words left his mouth Blu slapped the little stone against the menhir and the goblins were gone.

'Where did they go?' Madelaine asked in astonishment.

Hubert was standing with his mouth open.

'Hu?' Madelaine asked, then gave him a gentle shake, 'Hubert? What happened, do you know?'

'They went back to fairy land,' Hubert whispered in awe. 'There's a way through the standing stones, like a doorway, and if–'

'May I see the diamonds please?' Madelaine interrupted him.

Hubert dug in his pockets and handed the goblin treasure to his wife without taking his eyes off of the menhir.

'If we could find a way through … If we had one of those little stones …'

'No! Oh no more big rocks *please*, Hubert?' Madelaine begged. Then she let out a peal of laughter, 'Oh my love! We're rich! We can get the boat fixed, and we can afford to eat at the tavern some nights if we want. Oh my goodness, I could get a new dress! A red one, I've always wanted a red dress!'

Hubert laughed as he saw Madelaine's eyes fill with happy tears.

'I think you could have a great deal more than *one* new dress, love! Oh, and we can finally get *wedding rings,* we can have them made from one of the gold coins!'

Madelaine gave a little shriek of delight and jumped up and down before wincing at how sore her feet were.

'You should take me dancing more often,' she said, embracing him.

'We can go dancing whenever you like now, only … maybe not for a week or so until my blisters heal? I'm so exhausted,' Hubert added, holding her close.

'Oh, Hubert! You haven't slept at all. Come on, let's get your boots off and put you to bed.'

Hubert woke with a smile to the sound of happy humming. A ghost of the magical tune that the goblins had been singing the night before, except that it was in Madelaine's quiet voice.

'Good morning, my lady wife,' he said with a yawn, 'what are you up to?'

Madelaine looked up from what she was doing and smiled.

'I've been down to the shore and now I'm polishing our coppers.'

Hubert sat up and saw that Madelaine had gathered a little pile of brightly coloured shells and a piece of quartz. Next to them were the little pile of copper coins they had brought with them, formerly all their worldly wealth, now polished to a high shine so that they looked freshly minted.

'*Treasure,*' Madelaine explained.

'For the goblins?'

'Yes, I'm going to leave it by the menhir for those horrid little creatures. They've made me so happy that I feel I should do something for them in return.'

'Well, I don't mind making a journey here to leave some shiny things for them once in a while. It seems the least that we can do is to make them feel like they got a good deal.'

'Exactly! I shall buy them some pretty glass beads too,' Madelaine stood and danced over to the menhir, scattering shiny objects all around its base, before calling out, 'Hurry and get up, Hu! I want to go home and start spending all of our money on frivolous luxuries, like clothes and food. And then we can start living happily ever after.'

THE PRINCE AND THE PRINCESS

The storm raged with such fury that Brendan had no hope of steering the ship. They had lowered the sails and lashed the ship's wheel. Now the crew clung, soaked and shivering, to the mast and the rails. The rain beat down so heavily that it was hard for Brendan to keep his eyes open to watch the surging sea ahead.

Their ship, the *Sea Wolf*, had been bound for Jersey and the harbour at Goodnight Bay when the storm had darkened above them and unleashed itself with a roar of thunder. While they were probably hopelessly off course, there was nothing the young Captain could do, except offer up a silent prayer that they would not find themselves capsized. There were, counting crew and passengers, twenty-three souls aboard.

Brendan had lashed himself to the ship's wheel and clung on with grim determination, his clothes and short dark hair soaked against his cold skin. He heard other men being sick, but terror had turned his own stomach to a hard knot. As lightning tore the sky, Brendan strained his deep blue eyes to see whether there were rocks ahead, but could hardly see past the wolf's head prow. The storm-lashed rain twisted into shapes before his eyes, faces and figures in the wind, as though some malicious force drove the tempest. He felt very small afloat upon a raging ocean, at the mercy of nature's fickle fury as the storm song howled.

Lightning flashed another jagged white rip in the sky. The harsh light froze the scene into a monochrome image that burned against his retinas. The harrowed faces of his men and the towering waves were a still vision before his eyes whether they were closed or open, defiantly motionless despite the sickening pitch and yaw of the ship.

He blinked, shaking his head until the image began to fade, and assumed that a tiny point of light dancing in the distance was nothing more than the imprint upon his retinas. The ship lurched and heaved, dipping into the trough of a wave twice as high as the mast, and then reared upwards to crest the wall of water and hang in the air for one sickening moment before it slammed down again. Timbers creaked and moaned as though the ship itself were a living thing, and Brendan wondered how much more his *Sea Wolf* could take before she was torn apart. Fair weather had been predicted and expected. He had made certain. He always made certain.

Brendan saw again the point of light and then, as lightning danced overhead once more, the dark outline of land above the roiling waves.

'Land ahoy!' first mate Trevor Flynn's shout was almost lost in the roar of the wind.

'God help us,' Brendan whispered as the ship pitched with a stomach-churning lurch and spun about, lifting from the stern, almost vertical as a wave broke over the deck. Brendan heard a man scream as he was swept away, the sound abruptly cut off as he was submerged. He had no sense of north or south as the ship spun about again, no idea now of where they were in relation to the jagged shore. Direction was almost irrelevant since he could not hope to steer against the power of the ocean. He was struggling simply to hang on to the ship's wheel in order to avoid being washed overboard. Brendan risked raising his cold-stiffened fingers to his waistcoat pocket and felt the familiar shape of the gold ring which he carried, still safe from the storm. It was an engagement ring for his betrothed, Colleen. Brendan wondered whether he would ever see her again.

Lightning exploded, flash and thunder as one, and Brendan saw the cliffs rearing ahead once more. They would surely be dashed against the rocks as the storm pushed them closer.

It was then that he saw her. The source of the dancing light was a girl, holding a lantern as she leapt, graceful as a cat, over the rocks at the base of the cliff. Brendan thought that perhaps she was calling to them. There was an eerie sweetness on the wind, a sound that had not been there before.

A racking impact tore his grip from the wheel and only the ropes lashing him to it prevented him from being thrown like a rag doll. The ship bucked like a wild thing and the sound and explosion of cracking wood told him they had struck rocks. A great wave lifted them away and hurled them closer to the cliffs.

They would be taking on water now, Brendan realised. The bowels of the ship would fill, and they would be dragged down. Those sailors not pulled under in its wake would fight the waves until their strength gave out or their bodies were smashed and torn against the jagged rocks.

Brendan found himself lying almost flat on the wooden wheel as the wolf's head prow plunged down. He saw one of his men overboard, the man's face as pale as death. For an instant, Brendan thought he could almost reach out and touch the man's hand. It was Ethan, he realised, and then the swell lifted the ship and Ethan was lost.

He glimpsed the dancing light again. He saw beyond the lantern to the woman who held it. Her hair as white as sea-foam, long and silken, whipping wet about her in the storm. A thin soaked dress of pale green clung to her body. Her slender arms reached out to him and he felt a desperate need to reach the shore. He briefly considered untying the rope that bound him to the wheel and diving overboard to try to swim to her, but sanity prevailed.

'*Come to me*,' she called and her voice was the voice of the wind. She ran and sprang from the rocks, and Brendan realised that she had reached a small, pebbled beach, a narrow safe harbour between two threatening cliffs of dark stone.

Pulling his knife from his boot, Brendan sawed at the wet ropes that lashed the wheel. It came free with a spinning force that nearly threw him to the deck. With a strength Brendan did not know he had left, he took the helm. The wheel fought him like a possessed creature as the ship lurched starboard towards the cliffs.

His eyes searched for the woman. She stood, soaked and windblown, knee deep in the surf, arms wide as though awaiting his embrace.

'*Come to me,*' her voice was almost a song, so full of life. Her full, red lips promised safety, warmth, and so much more. She longed for him; he could hear it in her voice.

A sailor ran past Brendan, sliding on the wet deck, almost falling as he kicked off his boots and dove headfirst into the sea. The wolf's head prow lifted on a wave and then crushed him as it fell.

'*Come to me, come to me, come to me …*'

Her head was thrown back, rivulets of water running down her neck, between her breasts and down her legs as the sea spray whipped around her.

Brendan hauled on the wheel, crying out with the effort to pull the rudder round.

'*Come to me, come to me now!*'

The ship shuddered against the tide and began a sluggish turn. Too late perhaps. The waves were forcing the stern around, threatening to broadside them against the cliffs.

'*Turn* you bastard!' Brendan shouted, and somehow the ship began to edge closer to the beach. He could see the woman so clearly now, her parted lips wet with rain, her long legs barely concealed by the diaphanous film of her gown. Every curve of her pale body was visible and her eyes seemed to burn with a cold fire. There was a flash of lightening, and he could see that her eyes were the rich blue-green of the treacherous ocean. She was as pale as a corpse, like a woman recently drowned. She must be so cold. He would not trust the boat to make shore. He would swim to her.

Thoughts of Colleen were lost like a distant dream as the storm-song whispered and roared. As Brendan released the wheel, the prow drove into the shore beneath the waves and tilted the back end of the boat sharply to the right, where it smashed into the rocks at the base of the cliffs. The impact threw Brendan forcefully from the ship into the surf. There was a shock of cold and the thunder of water in his ears as he was submerged. He reared above the surface, blinking seawater from his eyes and tossing his dark hair from his

face, to see the ship wallowing towards him. Choking and fighting
the current, Brendan turned and kicked out, but the receding waves
dragged him back. His foot struck slippery shingle beneath him and
he managed to halt his progress, then was thrown forwards as a new
wave broke around him, knocking him off his feet. He swallowed
water and came up coughing, struggling forward against the erratic
drag and push of the current, wet stones sliding treacherously under
his boots.

The ship groaned behind him with a tearing of timbers. Glancing
back Brendan saw it bear down inexorably to crush him and, as he
flinched back, the prow slammed again into the beach and halted.
The snarling wooden wolf's figurehead stopped mere inches from
his face. With a gasp something like a laugh, Brendan turned and
forged through the water towards dry land. A body knocked against
his thighs and Brendan hooked his fingers in the man's collar before
he could be washed away. He dragged the body ashore as he staggered from the clinging tide and fell to his knees upon the wet black
pebbles of the beach in exhaustion.

The man he had pulled from the water, one of the passengers,
began to choke and vomit. Brendan looked for the pale woman
who had led them onto land. Over to his left she stood, arms still
held out to the waves as men struggled through the surf towards
her. She withdrew from the water, pushing past the bodies of the
dead and drowning, ignoring the calls of those who could not swim.
Bodies churned in the waves, their loose limbs flailing like unstrung
marionettes.

A slim and pale young man sat cross-legged upon a large, flat
stone behind her. The white stone lay like a fallen monolith, stark
against the black pebbles of the beach. Brendan only noticed him
when the man casually unfolded and hopped down from his perch.
Careless of the finery he wore, the young man waded without haste
into the ocean and began pulling living men and bodies onto the
beach. He lifted much larger men than himself with ease and
dumped each sailor unceremoniously onto the dark shingle before
moving onto the next.

One exhausted sailor reached the woman on his hands and knees. He grasped at her legs, fingers fumbling weakly at the thin cloth of her gown. Imbued with a sudden strength born of jealousy and outrage, Brendan struggled to his feet and strode forward, stones crunching under his boots, to cuff the man hard to the ground.

'My Lady,' he whispered, sinking to his knees before the woman, 'my name is Brendan Wolf. You saved me. You saved us all.'

She looked down at him with her cold eyes and laughed as though he had said something deeply amusing.

'I like wolves,' she said, her intoxicating voice crashing against him like a warm wave.

Brendan caught her hand to his lips and kissed her icy fingers fervently. It was not enough. Nothing would ever be enough. Passion overwhelmed convention and he stood to take her in his arms. Her beauty was flawless. Her features were so fine they seemed carved from ice by the hand of a master. Her eyes, snow lashed, were cold as the storm-torn sea. She wore no ornament save a simple necklace of white ribbon with a carved stone pendant. Her mouth, red as a fresh wound, was curved with an inviting smile.

Brendan's memories of Colleen became nothing more than a persistent tickle at the back of his mind. The promises they had sworn and the words of love that they had exchanged seemed so foolish as he stared into the ocean depths of this woman's turquoise eyes. He kissed her cold mouth with carnal force, pulling her lean body against his. He felt a sharp pain in his mouth and could taste his blood where she had bitten him. He was grateful for her savagery.

He drew back again to look at her, to glory in her. Her red mouth smiled wide at him. His blood was on her chin and glossy on her needle-sharp teeth.

A sudden harsh kick to the back of his knees caused him to fall, striking his head on the stony ground. He lay stunned, face-up upon the black pebbles.

'Brother,' the woman said reproachfully to the pale youth who stood above Brendan with contempt in his eyes.

'Don't play with your food, Selene,' responded the man languidly. Leaning in, he kissed her gently and licked Brendan's blood from her lips. 'Leave this silly child and help me with the others,' he added.

Dazed, Brendan watched as the pale brother and sister worked together to pull the living and the dead from the sea. When one of the sailors struggled against the pale brother's grasp, the youth lunged forward and sunk his sharp teeth into the man's throat. The sailor soon became still.

Selene lifted grown men without effort, her lean arms dealing easily with the dead weight of corpses and the grasping hands of the living. Many of them reached for Selene passionately and she would kiss them hard until they fell away, bloodied and stupefied. Brendan burned with jealousy even as his body shivered violently. He was wet and chilled and the dying wind cut through his sodden clothing like a cold knife.

His mouth was numb where Selene had bitten him. His face tingled and he could not find the strength to stand or even to stir. He wanted to go to the woman, to explain his sudden love for her, but the strange paralysis would not leave his body.

The storm died as swiftly as it had risen and dawn crept in cold and grey. The waves calmed as the pale brother and sister worked. Brendan could see them from time to time at the corner of his vision, moving out of view as they carried sailors away across the rocks and then returned. For the most part, he simply gazed upwards at the cold sky and the hills. Storm crows hung upon the dying wind, their raucous calls softened by the hiss of the surf. The burnt red of the dry heather and the shape of the black and red cliffs above began to seem familiar. They were, he realised, very near their original destination. He was lying on a small beach beneath the modest cliffs of Sorel Point in the north of the island. They were just along the coast from the *Sea Wolf*'s intended destination of Goodnight Bay, what the French-speaking people of Jersey called Bonne Nuit. He was within walking distance of La Fontaine Tavern, where he and his crew often stopped for mulled cider. They were probably only swimming distance from the caves that he and his crew used for storing their precious smugglers' cargo. Cargo that was now scattered or smashed beneath the waves. His ship was destroyed and his livelihood was gone. His crew were dead and dying in the water, but if Selene would only kiss him again then it would all be worth it.

Hands slid beneath his back and his view tilted suddenly as he was lifted by strong arms and carried like a newborn baby. He was jolted and jogged without consideration by the pale man who had picked him up. Brendan's unnatural stupor had left him without even the strength to lift his head or to protest. He winced as Selene's brother hopped up onto the rocks at the base of the cliff and made his way along with the same unnatural ease as his sister. Brendan squeezed his eyes shut, expecting at any moment to be dropped carelessly on the jagged volcanic rock.

Then he was thrown. There was a horrifying moment of weightless disorientation, and then the shock of chill water closed over Brendan's head in an explosive roar. His hands gave a reflexive spasm, but his muscles would not cooperate. He sank down, holding his breath, then began to rise slowly towards the surface, the air in his lungs making him buoyant. The burst of terrified adrenaline rushing through his veins allowed him to make the merest twitch of his limbs. It was barely enough to reach the surface but somehow his face reached the air and he exhaled explosively, inhaled, and sank beneath again. As the bubbles cleared around him Brendan saw a tangle of limbs in the dark water. The bodies of other sailors. As he floated to the surface he saw, through stinging eyes, that he had not been cast back into the ocean, but rather into a large, deep, rectangular rock pool cut into the face of the cliff. Whether it had been carved by the hand of man, or by nature, or by something else, he could not be sure. It was filled now with an horrific soup of dead and dying men.

Brendan tried to cry out. He could only rasp weakly in his throat before he sank again. He was helpless under the blue water and the slow churn of corpses. The air burned in his lungs. His foot had become caught in the clothing of someone dead beneath him and as his body lifted towards the light, it anchored him. If he only had the power to flex his legs he would be free, but even with the frantic terror of death upon him he could not find his strength.

Water filled his nose and mouth. Darkness began to narrow his vision and then a silhouette moved above him. A pale hand reached down, wrapped itself in his short hair, and hauled him from the water.

'... ever just *listen* to me, Arian?' Selene was saying with annoyance. 'I told you I wished to keep this one for a while. He's a pretty toy, don't you think?'

Spluttering and gasping as he was dumped onto the rocks, Brendan was aware that the pale man was regarding him with something less than admiration in his eyes.

'Oh really, brother! Tell me that you aren't jealous?'

Arian snorted, 'He's hardly a fitting consort for a Princess, sister. I won't take away your pet drowned rat, but you can carry him up to the stones yourself if you wish to take him home alive. I grow weary of hauling these creatures. There are enough here, I think, to keep us well fed for a while.'

'I agree,' she rested Brendan on the rocks and brushed his wet, dark hair back from his forehead. 'There now,' she said, 'you will come back to my home with me. You would like that, wouldn't you?'

Brendan's heart ached with fear and joy. She laughed as she saw these things in his blue eyes and showed her wicked teeth.

Turning back to her brother, she went on, 'There are a few on the beach who are awake enough to judge if you wish to play now, Arian.'

'This was a fine harvest.'

'Then your greys may eat their fill for once, Arian.'

'Call the Ouathou then, Selene,' the pale man smiled, 'he prefers his meat fresh, and screaming, but be sure to tell him your little rat is off limits,' he laughed, a sound like ice cracking.

The Princess gave an exasperated laugh, took a deep breath, and throwing back her head let out a wailing howl. The sound of it made Brendan tremble to the core; made him want to curl into a ball and hide his face in his hands. It reached deep inside him and touched a place of terror, which he had locked away with childhood fears, huddled under blankets on dark nights when the floorboards creaked and his dreams were filled with monsters. If her voice before had been the language of the storm, it was something altogether more horrible and bestial now. He managed a soft gasp and then another as his face was gripped suddenly in her hard, gaunt fingers.

'Did I scare you, my toy?' she said softly. 'No, hush, I know you cannot speak. You will regain your strength soon enough.'

The brother and sister moved away back towards the beach, swift with inhuman grace. Shadows moved in the trees along the edge of the beach, but Brendan did not think they were men.

Howls that were a hollow echo of the woman's voice rose from the trees. A violent shivering began to wrack Brendan's body as wolves emerged from the green shadows. The beasts were almost twice the size of any that he had seen before. The wolf pack were grey except for four that were pure white. The wolves began to fall on the men by the shore, the dead and the dying, tearing at them like starving dogs as the Prince and Princess walked among them. A huge creature, the size of a bear and walking upright like a man, followed the others. It paused to regard the wallowing wolf's head prow of Brendan's shattered ship, then dipped its huge head and began to feast on the body of one of the living sailors.

Finding he finally had the power to move his head, Brendan looked away and closed his eyes, but he could not shut out the screams. He must save Selene from this, he decided. She surely could not understand the horror that she was a part of.

'Captain,' an urgent voice whispered, and then more loudly, 'damn it, Brendan, open your eyes.'

Brendan blinked and squinted around until he saw Trevor Flynn, a man who had been an old hand at sailing since before Brendan had been born.

'Here, lad,' Trevor's voice was shaky. He was floating, face-up, as though drowned in the pool, but his eyes were bright, and his fist was clenched tightly around the silver hilt of his dagger, its blade almost out of sight beneath the water.

'I'm going to have to make a run for it, lad,' Trevor said in a grim whisper. 'The time for playing dead is done. They have a thrall on you, boy, so I can't take you with me. God knows I wish I could. You're as good a captain as any I've sailed with, and you got us to shore, but I don't see as I can help you now,' the old sailor lifted his head until he saw the wolves and he grimaced.

'Young Trent went for help the second we reached land. He knows this island. He headed for the monastery at Don Farm.'

The words made sense to Brendan, but he could not respond except to blink at the old sailor a few times.

'Good luck to you, Captain,' Trevor Flynn said, and with a speed that belied his age, he hauled himself from the pool in a rush of water and was up and scaling the rocks at the base of the hill towards the steep grassy slope above.

For a few seconds it seemed as though no creature on the beach had noticed the old sailor, and then suddenly a wolf was running, then another, then a third. Their muzzles were already red with blood, but a prone meal was nowhere near as appealing as one that could be hunted. The Ouathou raised its head, blood dripping from its jaws.

Arian and Selene were stood on the white monolith, with a sailor on his knees at their feet. Arian's sword was drawn and Brendan watched him run it through the chest of the sailor and then kick him aside distractedly. Both the brother and sister stepped gracefully from the white sacrificial stone to watch the pursuit.

The grey wolves reached the rocks and closed upon the old sailor. They passed Brendan in a ragged scratching of claws upon stone, jaws slathering bloody drool, and caught up with Trevor Flynn in a matter of moments. Turning in his tracks, Flynn sank into a fighting crouch, his silver dagger slashing wildly at the first creature to reach him. A yelp, like the sound of a kicked dog, told Brendan that the old man's knife had made contact.

'That's right, you monsters!' Trevor shouted, his voice frail with fear. 'A silver blade. I've dealt with fae filth before.'

The wolves began to circle, snarling, and Trevor had to twist and whirl to keep each in view as they whipped in from every side. They slid out of reach of his dagger just in time, each looking for an opportunity to reach him while he was distracted. It was just a matter of time, Brendan realised, before they had Flynn down.

Brendan tried to struggle against the torpor in his own limbs and found that he could clench and unclench his hands, but beyond that he could not force his body to respond. He swore in hoarse frustration, and in doing so found he had regained the power of speech.

The huge wolf-creature called the Ouathou, and the pale Prince and Princess, moved without haste back towards them with the curious expressions of spectators at a show.

Old Flynn had somehow managed to back himself up against the thorns of one of the twisted gorse-bushes on the hill, protecting his back, but leaving him without hope of further retreat.

Brendan cowered as the Ouathou stalked past. Its huge clawed hands were the size of dinner plates. Trevor Flynn and his silver dagger seemed absurdly small and frail as the Ouathou approached him. With a sound like rock grinding against rock, the creature growled.

'Come any closer and you'll lose an eye, you filthy mutt,' Flynn cried out, his voice thin with terror. He held his silver dagger out before him now more like a ward than a weapon.

The Ouathou lifted a huge claw, and then recoiled with a roar as though struck. A wolf yelped and stumbled to the ground, whining, with an arrow jutting from its side. Brendan saw the first arrow in the Ouathou's shoulder before its monstrous claw clamped around it in a fist and ripped it out.

Arrows fell amongst the wolves as Trent and a group of black-robed monks came into view on the beach. All were armed with bows. Trent was just a cabin boy, barely into his teens, yet he waded into battle with the wolves on the shingle with the vigour of a seasoned warrior.

'Good lad!' Brendan heard Trevor Flynn shout, and he felt his own numb and bloodied lips curve in a smile.

A vicious hiss sounded from beside him and Brendan looked up to see Selene's face distorted with hatred.

'Silver-tipped arrows? How quaint,' she spat.

Her brother was beside her suddenly.

'Time to leave, sister,' he said without any particular show of concern, 'leave the rat, will you?'

'No,' the Princess snarled, 'I'll not be cheated of my toy.'

For the second time, Brendan found himself yanked upwards and carried, as Selene threw him over her shoulder. The Prince and Princess made their way with swift ease towards the base of the hill, then began to climb.

Wolves scattered into the trees from the beach or raced ahead of the unhurried Ouathou as they scaled the hill. Silver arrows killed some, and as they died, their bodies warped and twisted. Some fell to the ground as dead men, others became the bodies of more distorted humanoid shapes.

Brendan heard a cry of dismay from Trevor Flynn and then Trent's high voice from the beach as the boy realised, 'They have the Captain!'

The Prince and Princess did not increase their speed. Their fluid grace was too swift for the men racing from the beach to catch them. Twisting his neck, Brendan watched idly as the monks swarmed onto the rocks in pursuit. His head whirled with vertigo as he hung upside down over his lady's shoulder, looking down over the steep incline.

Flynn's face was a mask of dismay. Brendan wished he could have explained to the man that he needed to be with the Princess. Perhaps even, he thought with a tiny flash of guilt, ask Flynn to take a message to his fiancé explaining that he could not go through with the wedding. He had thought he loved Colleen until today. He would have sworn even as the storm began that he had never cared as much for another woman.

They had reached the top of the hill and Brendan was dumped as unceremoniously as a sack of potatoes against a dolmen of upright white stones. They were nothing like the natural blush-coloured granite of the cliffs and looked, like the fallen monolith of white stone upon the beach, to be from a different place entirely.

'My poor dear brother,' the Princess said idly, 'we barely even had time for you to start your judgement games.'

'There will be other times,' the Prince said with a shrug as he patted himself down in exasperation. 'Where is the damn thing?' he muttered, then gave a satisfied exclamation as he pulled what, at Brendan's first glance, appeared to be a pebble from his jacket pocket.

Arian held it up triumphantly and Brendan saw that it was a pendant similar to the stone necklace that Selene wore, only with a different symbol.

The sounds of pursuit grew louder as the monks struggled up the steep hill towards the dolmen. They were just appearing over the crest of the hill as the Prince used his free hand to clasp his sister's and they moved to stand over Brendan. Selene took Brendan's hand and he sighed with pleasure.

Then there was a sound like a fist hitting flesh and Arian's body contorted suddenly. Selene gave an unearthly shriek as her brother dropped to his knees and leant against the white stone with a grimace of pain. Brendan saw the feathered shaft of an arrow jutting from the man's lower back. Blood as dark as claret spread into the fine, pale fabric of his clothes as he hissed with discomfort.

'Touch the stone,' Selene commanded, and tearing the silken thong from her neck she slammed the stone ornament of her necklace against the white rock of the dolmen.

Brendan did as he was bid, and experienced a sensation like falling. He grasped desperately at the Princess's hand, but in an instant it was over and the monks had disappeared.

'Where did they go?' Brendan mumbled in surprise.

'Nowhere,' the Princess said, 'it was we who departed.'

She bent down to tend to Arian and snapped the feathered quill from the arrow. Grasping the point of the arrow where it jutted from her brother's stomach, she wrenched it through his body and flung it away in disgust.

'Those wretched fools!' snarled the Prince with a fury that made Brendan recoil away from him.

'What?' The Princess laughed, gently touching her bloodied hand to Arian's cheek. 'It is but a bee sting to you, brother.'

'It knocked my key from my hand!'

Brendan looked around for the stone pendant the Prince had been holding, saying, 'But it can't have gone far.'

'It's not here, you fool! It's on the other side,' Arian raised his hand, fingers twisted into a claw.

'Are you sure?' The Princess caught the Prince's hand before he could strike Brendan.

'It's not here,' Arian shouted with a hint of petulance.

Glancing around, the Princess appeared to realise that he was right. She began to curse in a manner that caused Brendan's mouth to fall open.

'No matter!' she exclaimed eventually, 'We will go back for it. But not now. I don't wish to be riddled with arrows.'

'You could sing the men down,' Arian suggested.

'Not if they have silver, brother,' she said gently, kneeling beside the Prince. 'Do not fuss. They will not realise what your key is, and we still have the Angon,' she said, holding up her own stone necklace.

'Now come Arian, it has been a long night and you are bleeding.'

Selene hauled Brendan up and turned him around. Before, where there had been nothing on the pinnacle of the hill, there stood a white tower.

'Welcome to your new home, Brendan Wolf,' Selene said softly.

Trent cried out in horror as the Captain and his captors disappeared. Old Flynn, struggling for breath, fell to his knees and began to gasp in ragged breaths, exhausted from the climb.

'I am sorry,' said one of the monks quietly.

'Where did they go?' demanded Trent. 'They disappeared! Where did they go?'

'They've gone back to the land of the fae, lad,' Trevor Flynn wheezed, 'through the old stones. Captain's lost to us now. He wouldn't come back even if he could. He was under a thrall. It's only that silver St Nicholas necklace around your neck which stopped the same thing happening to you.'

'But why?' The boy shook his head in confusion, 'Why did they take him?'

'Who knows,' Flynn said, sitting back on his heels, 'who knows why the fae do the things they do? I've never seen the like of that though. Never in all my years …'

Flynn fell quiet and simply shook his head while staring out to sea.

'The Prince and the Princess are a curse upon this place,' one of the monks said quietly.

'Then why don't you do something about them?' Trent demanded. He took slow steps up to the white stone dolmen and regarded it with distrust.

'We do not know how to follow where they have gone,' the monk said, 'their methods and means are beyond us. They move through the old stones as though they were a doorway and, when they vanish, whatever is below in the cursed pool vanishes with them.'

Flynn shuddered as he considered how recently he had been floating in that same pool. 'Lost to us,' he repeated to himself as he hauled himself up and slowly made his way to Trent's side.

'We should tear these things down and throw them off the damn cliff,' said Trent, spitting on the dolmen.

A glint of light off a smooth stone caught Flynn's eye and the old sailor bent down with a grunt and picked up a strangely shaped pebble on a chain. There was a design carved into the surface, but Flynn's old eyes being what they were, he could not quite make it out. He thought

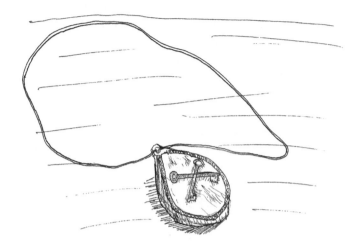

that perhaps it might be the stone that the Princess had been wearing around her neck. He weighed it in his hand and smiled grimly.

'Let's do that then,' Flynn growled, 'let's pull it down.'

Turning, Flynn threw the pendant with all of his strength, casting it far and high so that it arched out over the cliff face and, without a sound, was swallowed by the sea.

∽

Arian's pendant remained lost in the darkness of the ocean depths for over five hundred years. The drag and surge of the tides lifted and dropped the Stone Key to rest within a shallow crevice of cold, black rock deep beneath the surface. The persistent motion of the ocean wore down and carried away the white stone monolith and the remains of the dolmen that had been cast down by survivors from the *Sea Wolf*. Yet centuries slipped by and the Stone Key did not stir in the darkness. The chain attached to it rusted and fell away, but the carved impression of two crossed keys upon its surface remained unworn and undiminished by the constant caress of the churning tides. It glittered weakly in the light refracted through the silent, heavy fathoms.

Over time the world grew warmer as human industry slowly poisoned the skies and the sea level began to rise. Next to Sorel Point a quarry was established to cut the valuable pink Jersey granite from the cliffs. The landscape of the island changed dramatically and altered the rush and surge of the rising tides as the currents shifted around the coast.

On the night of a full moon, on a spring tide storm as powerful as any tempest raised by the Prince and Princess, the surf churned to a rage. At its highest point the heaving sea tore the Stone Key free from its resting place and flung it twirling back into the embrace of the moving ocean.

Whispering waves lifted the pendant, spinning and glittering in the water, and gradually, relentlessly, the tide began to wash the forgotten Stone Key back towards the shore.

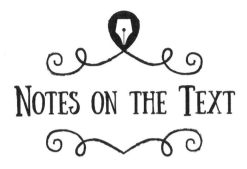

Notes on the Text

✆ SIR HAMBIE AND THE DRAGON ✆

I first heard the tale of Sir Hambie and the Dragon from a friend, who was a member of a cast performing the story as a comic play for a village fête. She was playing the part of Sir Hambie's wife. Sir Hambie (more properly Seigneur Hambye in the legend) was played by our appropriately named friend Michael Hanby.

The story of Sir Hambie, while not very well known, is certainly more widely recorded than most Jersey fairy tales and has several versions. There was even a novel published in 1896 called *The Knight and the Dragon*, which retells the story with a great deal of embellishment and a pervasive theme of Christian forgiveness, yet omits any description of the battle itself.

An image depicting the battle between the knight and the dragon also appeared on two Jersey stamps in their 'Folklore' series in 1981 under the title 'A Legend of La Hougue Bie'. J.H. L'Amy in his book *Jersey Folk Lore* theorises that the legend may actually have some basis in historical fact, quoting E.T. Nicolle's writing in the *Bulletin Société Jersiaise* that, 'The dragon was the symbol of Paganism in the Christian cult, and Knights who slew a Pagan Chief in battle were considered to have slain a dragon,' (*Jersey Folk Lore*, p. 38).

However, this Jersey legend also bears marked resemblance to the more famous Norse legend of Sigurd the Slayer, in which Sigurd slays the dragon Fafnir. During that battle a drop of Fafnir's magical blood falls into Sigurd's mouth. The dragon's blood gives Sigurd the power to understand the language of the animals, and enables him to hear the warning from two birds that his own disloyal companion, the evil dwarf Regin, plans to murder him. Sigurd swiftly kills Regin and avoids Sir Hambie's tragic fate.

᧥ THE BLACK DOG OF BOULEY BAY ᧥

The Black Dog tavern has stood for centuries, and its name is a constant reminder of the legend from which it takes its name. Perhaps ironically it was the trade of alcohol itself that caused smugglers to appropriate tales of the black dog. They used stories and costumes to scare people away from their illicit activities, and thus made the legend famous.

There are tales of the black dog breathing fire and attacking fishermen, or dragging a chain behind him. He seems to have a reputation as a storm herald, but there are also accounts of sightings in which he has been sitting peacefully beside the road.

The black dog of Bouley Bay is only one of a number of supernatural black dogs that are rumoured to exist in the island. The black dog as an image seems to crop up in folklore with extraordinary regularity: as a storm warning, as a treasure guardian or as a Grimm, a harbinger of misery and death.

With such a well-known phantom and no one specific legend to describe him, I tried to use elements from Jersey history to create something that allowed the black dog to retain his mysterious nature and yet touched upon the smugglers' use of the legend that helped to immortalise the creature in Jersey folklore.

❧ THE VIOGE ❧

La Ruette à la Vioge is a very steep and narrow footpath in St Peter that stretches between the area of Sandybrook and Wheatlands and is, according to the legend, the hunting ground of a singular monster in Jersey folklore.

The Vioge seems to have no real similarity to any other archetypal creature in myth and cannot easily be categorised as a specific type of monster. In his book *Jersey Folklore*, J.H. L'Amy quotes an older source, 'Vioge is an old French word, meaning "ghost" – something that frightens and corresponds to the patois word "émânue", a scarecrow' (*Jersey Folklore*, p. 177). From L'Amy we also learn that the Vioge was rumoured to have a cave where it would carry its victims to consume them.

G.J.C. Bois in his book speculates that the dialectal origins of the word 'vioge' itself might mean it has connotations such as 'listless' or 'lacking in energy' (*Jersey Folklore and Superstitions: Volume 2*, p. 2).

∞ SACRED GROUND ∞

Almost certainly one of the oldest legends in the island, the tale of the fairies and St Brelade's church may date back as far as AD 800 when the fishermen's chapel was built. The ancient church itself was started in AD 1200 and has had renovations and extensions throughout the centuries. It remains a strikingly beautiful piece of architecture in a location of outstanding natural beauty.

The comic poem 'The Legend of St Brelade's Church' from Thomas Williams' *Jersey Legends in Verse*, published in 1865, provides a version of the tale in which the fairies tie down Monsieur Grondin the overseer like the Lilliputians in *Gulliver's Travels*. His indignity is compounded when tiny Queen Mab drives her chariot over his face.

Other versions have the fairies or 'le petits faîtchieaux' carrying the stones away in their aprons unobserved by anyone. In this story I chose to include the White Lady (La Blianche Dame of Jersey folklore) an important and well-known figure in the mythology of the island who, while the equivalent of Queen Mab, has a more benevolent reputation and a more normal stature. While the White Lady of Jersey is included in local legend in various accounts of sightings and is associated with the menhirs and the pouquelaye standing stones or 'fairy stones', her mysterious nature means that no specific narrative myth is attached to her alone.

ഏൟ THE FIVE SPANISH SHIPS ഏൟ

The tale of 'The Five Spanish Barques' is another legend that has been recorded in many forms. The identity of the primary character changes in different versions, sometimes it is an old man begging to have his granddaughter saved, sometimes a mother with her child. Sometimes the curse of the great wave is immediate, but in most versions of the story it is fulfilled one year to the day after the ships were wrecked. It is unique in that it positions the people of Jersey as the villains of the piece, touching upon the practice of the deliberate wrecking of ships in the treacherous area which now houses La Corbiere lighthouse. 'La Corbiere' in Jèrraise translates to 'The Raven' and I named the lead ship in the story for that reason.

Historically the legend seems to be placed around 1495, although what truth there may be in the story of a great wave destroying the land is uncertain.

It is difficult to look at St Ouen's Bay and not wonder how the landscape came to be shaped in the way that it is. A vast area of land far out of reach of the tide is covered in dunes of sand almost like a desert.

✑ WITCHES' ROCK ✑

Rocqueberg, known locally as Witches' Rock, is one of the few locations in the island which has two separate and distinct legends attached to it, both very well known. The huge rock, which juts up from the landscape, seems almost designed to spark the imagination; although in some cases, the legends seem to refer not to the breathtaking granite stone rising from the earth inland, but to an outcropping of rock along the shore.

I tried to encompass the simpler 'Tale of the Thirteenth Fish' (which Hubert describes to Madelaine) within the larger story of Madelaine's struggle to win her hapless fiancé back from the thralls of the witches. Like many Jersey legends, both tales originally concluded with the same predictable finale: witches are shown the sign of the cross, scream, and disappear.

While such stories may appear quaint, it is well to remember that conservative estimates place the number of those killed in Europe after being erroneously accused of witchcraft at around 50,000. Some historians believe the number of deaths to be in the millions. Innocent people, supposedly at least three quarters of them women, were tortured and put to death in the most horrific ways.

Like the rest of Europe, 'witchcraft' in the Channel Islands was treated with hysterical superstition. Records from the Jersey Royal Court record the sentences of people found guilty of 'sorcery' who were executed by such methods as hanging, strangulation and being burnt to death.

∾ THE WATER HORSE ∾

The legend of 'Le Cheval Guillaume' in Bonne Nuit Bay is another of the better-known fairy tales of Jersey. It was also by far the most problematic to write. No other legend varies so much in its disparate versions. Some interpretations of the tale have Anne-Marie or 'Anna' alone on the beach at the start. In some she is walking with her sister, or with a group of women. Some variations refer to the creature that attacks her as a demon, some specifically call it a kelpie.

Traditionally kelpies are natives of Celtic legend, and are evil fairy horses that charm their victims into mounting them before leaping into the water to drown them and eat their bodies. They are not shape-shifters possessed of speech in the manner of the demon of Bonne Nuit Bay who first appears.

Then there is the problem that in all earlier versions of the story, the monster is initially driven away either by the breaking light of day or the first crowing of a cockerel. However, later in the story, once in the form of the horse, the monster apparently has no problem walking around in the daylight.

In attempting to write a version of this particular legend that made logical sense, I came to wonder if the story as it is commonly told now may have been two separate fairy tales which have become cobbled together over time.

In some versions of the story, William, or Guillaume, has premonitions in the form of dreams that he must gather mistletoe. In another version the demon, or kelpie, seeks out the aid of an evil ghost to give him extra powers after he hears the lovers talking. In some he is a lone demon. In others he is one of a number of kelpies residing in Bonne Nuit Bay, but he is so disliked that none of the female kelpies or nixies will marry him. He then seeks a human bride to live beneath the waves with him. Presumably the obvious flaw in his plan would have become apparent once she had drowned.

✑ DEVIL'S HOLE ✑

Devil's Hole, in the cliffs of the parish of St Mary, is an impressive crater-like rock formation with a narrow passage that leads to the sea. The name Devil's Hole may have originated because of the impressive appearance of this natural open cave, or as a bastardisation of its original name, 'Le Creux de Vis' (the screw-hole) or even, as some theorise, because of the threatening sound of the waves roaring through the narrow passage at high tide. However, when the figurehead of the wreck *La Josephine* washed in through the cave entrance in 1851, the Devil's Hole found its resident demon.

A sculptor carved arms and legs for this original statue, but the wear and tear of the elements and instances of vandalism have meant that the devil has been replaced with newer versions a number of times. It has now been relocated from the Devil's Hole itself to a pond just outside of the car park of The Priory Inn.

The most recent devil is an impressive bronze casting of a huge satyr with a trident designed by sculptor Ian Bishop.

The historical events of the Devil's Hole shipwreck took place sometime around late October 1851. During the night the French vessel *La Josephine*, carrying a cargo of lamp oil, was wrecked either during a storm or in fog, depending on the account. Only one crewmember, Constant Pétibon, lost his life attempting to swim for shore.

The story I have written is an original fictionalisation inspired by the historical events of the shipwreck, the location, and the devil statue itself.

∞ THE CROOKED FAIRY ∞

As with the Vioge, there is almost no recorded information on the legend of the crooked fairy or Lé Croque-mitaine as he is named in Jèrraise. The name 'Crooked Fairy' itself indicates a certain body type and manner of movement. G.J.C. Bois's assertion that mention of the crooked fairy was still used to frighten children, 'as late as 1957' (*Jersey Folklore & Superstitions: Volume Two*, p. 19) indicates that this particular monster was certainly considered dangerous and frightening, at least by infants. The other main character of the story, that of the changeling Amory Harker, was inspired by the legends of changelings within the island. Local accounts of changelings are similar to those within Celtic mythology. In such tales, human babies are stolen and replaced with identical fairy children, who acted strangely, or who could be tricked into revealing their true nature as supernatural beings.

∞ GOBLIN GOLD ∞

Within this story I incorporated two separate legends from the island. The first is the myth that treasure can be found buried beneath the pouquelaye or 'fairy' stones, and probably originates from the discovery of coins or jewellery found within the burial chambers of the island's dolmens.

The second is that described by J.H. L'Amy, 'A fearsome race of goblins are said to inhabit the long upright stones, known as menhirs, and if you pass their abodes at midnight they will dance around you and make you imitate their movements until you die.' (*Jersey Folk Lore*, p. 19.)

⊚ THE PRINCE AND THE PRINCESS ⊚

The legend of 'The Prince and the Princess' originates at Sorel Point on the north coast of the island, and may have been inspired by the twin caves of the same name in that location. Alternatively the caves themselves may take their names from the tale.

In the original legend, the Prince would draw passing ships onto the rocks by lighting a fire. Survivors of the wrecks who made it to shore were 'judged' and found wanting by the Prince, who would slaughter them upon a sacrificial stone altar. The bodies of the dead would then be placed within the natural Venus pool located at the base of the cliffs before being transported away by boat.

The Princess seems to be an entirely passive character in the surviving details, serving no function within the myth. Her relationship to the Prince, whether as wife or sister, is unclear and there is no overt supernatural power credited to the two. A thorough deconstruction of the surviving myth, and many others, can be found in *Jersey Folklore and Superstitions: Volume One* by J.C.G. Bois.

Included within my version of the tale are elements of other supernatural legends associated with the north coast of Jersey, such as the tragic voices of the dead upon the wind from the legend of the Paternosters. These are a group of treacherous rocks which can be seen from Sorel Point and which were the site of a tragic wreck in which all lives were lost.

The character of Brendan Wolf has his name from Wolfs Caves (*sic*) just along the coast, which apparently took their title from a smuggler who used the caves to conceal his illicit cargo. Brendan Wolf's abduction touches upon the belief that the Jersey fairy land of Angia is somehow separate from the human world, as well as the fairy practice of stealing mortals away to their own land. The giant Ouathou werewolf is a Jersey myth in his own right, but again has no story attached to his legend. I imbued the (previously unnamed) Princess of this tale with the powers of the legendary sea goddess Ahès Dahut, a magician princess who is a part of the legends of nearby Brittany and Jersey's surrounding seas.

BIBLIOGRAPHY

P. Ahier, *Jersey Sea Stories* (La Haule Books, 1984)

G.J.C. Bois, *Jersey Folklore & Superstitions* (AuthorHouse, 2010)

S.J. Coleman, *Treasury of Folklore* (The Folklore Academy, 1954)

H. Gabourel, *The Knight and the Dragon: A Legend* (Hayes & Co., 1896)

S. Hillsdon, *Jersey Witches, Ghosts & Traditions* (Jarrold & Sons Ltd, 1984)

J.H. L'Amy, *Jersey Folk Lore* (La Haule Books, 1927)

Magnet Magazine, *The Bonne Nuit Kelpie* (1973)

M. Warner, *Once Upon a Time* (Oxford University Press, 2014)

T. Williams, *Jersey Legends in Verse* (Saunders, Otley & Co., 1865)

Also from The History Press

ANCIENT LEGENDS RETOLD

This series features some of the country's best-known folklore heroes. Each story is retold by master storytellers, who live and breathe these legends. From the forests of Sherwood to the Round Table, this series celebrates our rich heritage.

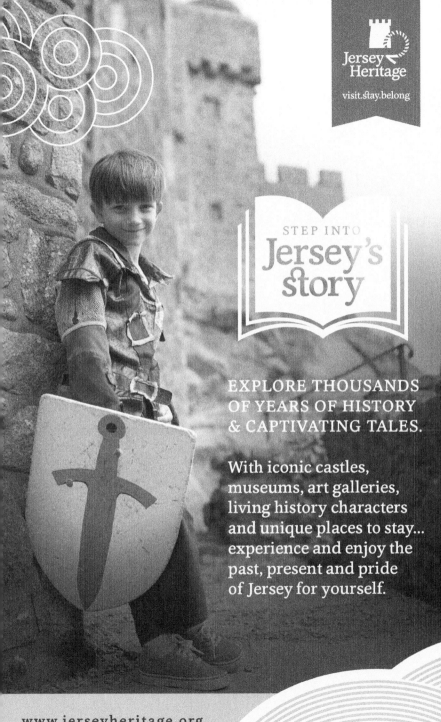

STEP INTO
Jersey's story

EXPLORE THOUSANDS OF YEARS OF HISTORY & CAPTIVATING TALES.

With iconic castles, museums, art galleries, living history characters and unique places to stay... experience and enjoy the past, present and pride of Jersey for yourself.

Jersey Heritage
visit.stay.belong

www.jerseyheritage.org

Lightning Source UK Ltd.
Milton Keynes UK
UKOW06f2302191115

263087UK00009B/148/P